Something New Every Day

The secret of the Garntuoas

Kin Asdi

CONTENTS

ACKNOWLEDGMENT

I spent many enjoyable evenings and weekends writing this
book and I loved the exciting interchange with my
copyeditor. This book would never have made it this far
without the humour and dedication of my fantastic
copyeditor, Ingrid Hall.
Thank you, Ingrid!
http://www.luv2write.net/

CHAPTER ONE.

Everyone on the street was desperately fighting to keep their umbrellas under control to prevent the slashing rain from penetrating their clothes. The wind was unpredictable and every gust of wind could cause an umbrella to flip over rendering it useless.

I didn't care if I got wet. I liked the rain; it was refreshing, sparkling on my skin and making me feel more awake on those dark days. I always had an urge to break out into fits of laughter, whenever I saw somebody fighting with an umbrella trying to turn it back to its original shape.

I was not a geek who went out just because it was raining, but I didn't mind when I was on my special mission. It made my mission a bit more exciting, because of the extra danger involved and the results were far more spectacular. I had been waiting for this opportunity for at least two months, and I knew that if I made the tiniest mistake it would result in disaster. Timing was crucial and on that day, in particular, I was counting on the dark clouds and heavy rain to hide and rinse away the evidence as quickly as possible.

I had counted the days and had everything neatly out

down on the table in my workroom. Every day I checked to see whether I needed to adjust my planning, but it was still a profitable opportunity with a very low risk.

Now the moment was there, and I double checked to see whether my specially designed blob gun was still functioning. It had failed me once before at a critical moment and this time I was taking no chances. In the nick of time, I managed to conceal my weapon from a passer-by who nodded in a friendly manner, clearly not suspecting anything.

After the last incident, it had taken me more than a month to fix the bloody thing again, and I had to undergo another dangerous trip to the crash side.

I still couldn't believe how lucky I had been in finding the place. I had been hiding in the wasteland because the authorities were far too interested in me, and it was then when I found the crash site of a strange vessel. The vessel was burned out completely, but there was a strange looking metal case that seemed to be pretty undamaged. With sheer brute force, I managed to gain access to the content of the case where I found a few weird looking devices. I came to the conclusion that they were of alien make. The blob gun was one of them.

At that moment, I didn't know what it was capable of but after a dozen experiments I figured it out. The only real challenge I had was in replacing the drained alien power pack with an ordinary battery pack. I nearly lost the bloody gun when the first converter caught fire. However, I am a quick learner, and now the blob gun has been my friend for many successful adventures.

The wind was howling above me when I turned into the small corridor between the two shops. I still didn't understand why the jewellery store didn't have this window reinforced. It was a piece of cake to make a nice big hole with the blob gun and take the beautifully crafted pieces of jewellery. I was grateful for the darkness as I aimed the blob gun at the window.

Looking around to make certain that no one was looking into the narrow corridor, I was startled by a woman standing in the window. Her beauty shook me. She had raven black hair that contrasted her pale complexion and I was reluctant to fire the gun. She looked at me with her grey-blue eyes as if she didn't believe what I was going to do.

I suddenly felt a charge of electricity shoot through me. My hair stood up on end as a sizzling thin strand of bright light shot up in the air from the blob gun. Lightning, surely!

I immediately threw the gun away as far as possible.

My heart was in my throat as I felt the static pull on my hair becoming bigger. I knew I was in deep shit, and the girl's eyes got bigger just before I saw the blinding flash.

I felt the shocking, intense, painful heat, and I blacked out completely.

****

As pieces of different fluffy pastel tinted strands flowed through the sky, I heard a male voice asking, "Why did you bring him here? His whole nerve system endured an enormous blast. You can't expect him to recover from such severe damage."

A young female voice answered, "I just couldn't leave him there suffering that badly. Can't you use anything else to fix him?"

The person sighed before saying, "I will take a look, but I honestly, fear the worst."

The strands started to hum loudly, and the sky thickened by the second as the voices overwhelmed me. The darkness descended rapidly as a peaceful nothingness brought order to the chaos.

~

My leg was twitching.
It stopped.

There! It was twitching again! Now it was my other leg making a forceful uncoordinated move.

Even though I couldn't move my arms, I felt remarkably relaxed.

Now both legs were trembling which was strange. The prickling sensation began to fade as I felt myself drop back into the nice warm darkness.

~

I was lying in the grass looking at the sky. I blinked my eyes to be sure that it was the sky I was looking at. The colour was slightly off because the sky was more yellow than blue. I tried to look around but was unable to move my body at all.

The face of a girl appeared in my field of vision. She smiled, and her two ponytails at each side of her head swung a little as she giggled.

With a soft voice she said, "I like the way you look at me."

I tried to say something, but my lips and my vocal cords stayed as they were. I was scared that I would be paralysed for the rest of my life. Her expression changed into a caring smile and said with a melodic voice, "Don't worry you are doing well. Have patience. You'll be fine."

As she disappeared from my vision, I started to feel lonely for the first time in my life. I was not sure for how long I had been staring at the yellow sky before I fell asleep.

~

The sky was green the next time I opened my eyes, and I noticed that my lips were extremely dry. I moved my tongue trying to moisten my lips and after a few minutes I had reached each corner of my lips with my tongue.

I heard footsteps in the grass, and I was amazed to hear the little crunching noises when the long stalks were trampled down. The girl's face appeared in the field of my vision again and with a pretty smile she said, "Hello."

Taking a deep breath, and I tried to reply with great

and painful effort, "H....lo."

I was shocked to hear my extremely croaky voice. She chuckled softly as if she had some compassion, but then she touched my cheek with her extremely soft and warm fingers and said, "I know it's hard, but you're doing extremely well. You've exceeded all expectations."

I needed a drink of water, and I tried to say the word, but my mouth and throat were too dry. I squeaked a little, and the girl said, "I know you want water, but you need to heal a bit more before you can drink fluids."

She dabbed my lips with a wet cloth that felt nice and cool. The burning sensation on my lips disappeared for a short while. Her fine beautiful face and her blue grey eyes were bringing me joy, and I just wanted to lose myself in her.

The girl looked away as if she had been called. With a somewhat sad face, she caressed my hair and said, "Try to sleep. You'll heal much faster if you're sleeping."

When she disappeared, I felt empty, and a choir of voices were bringing me down to the darkest fear I ever had experienced. The paralysing feeling of helplessness and the revolting dark was horrible. I was incapable of screaming, no matter how much I tried and tried.

****

When I next opened my eyes, I noticed that the sky had a hint of turquoise, and I briefly wondered why the sky changed colours every time I woke up. I had the feeling that I was not on Earth but a different planet. It was strange how I could remember the different colours the sky had had, but I couldn't remember anything else.

I felt strange as if something in my mind was fighting against a blockage. However, I wasn't disturbed by this. I felt comfortable and at ease even though something was nagging in the back of my mind, and I was pondering what it should be.

I was frustrated by the speed of my reasoning, which right now was incredibly slow.

I must have a name!

The fact I knew I must have a name gave me the feeling that something was off. But I didn't know what.

I longed to see the pretty girl again. She was curiously familiar to me. She had been changing as well. Subtle changes as if she was getting older much faster than...... Faster than what?

Her face looked so familiar.

What was going on?

I heard the soft crunching of the dried grass being trampled down, and I smiled when I saw the girl again. She had her hair in a ponytail, but there were two little strands of hair hanging down next to her ears. She looked me straight in the eye and said softly, "Hello."

This time my throat felt less dry, and I could say nearly without any effort, "Hello."

My voice was still harsh but not as bad as the last time. Her voice had changed as well, sounding more mature as if she had grown older in a very short period. "How do you feel?"

This question suddenly forced me to focus on me, and I had great difficulty feeling anything. I stammered, "I, I don't know."

Her face looked confused, and she asked, "Do you have any pain?"

I was shocked by her question. Why should I feel pain? As far I could feel anything I could feel no pain, except for my sore throat, and I answered her question placidly, "No I don't."

I was not happy that I didn't feel anything else, and I tried to focus on her because she was real. I asked, "What's your name?"

At first she looked shocked before relaxing and saying, "You're not supposed to ask someone's name. It's considered very rude."

"Sorry."

I was shocked that I just said sorry. Why should I say sorry? She smiled and said, "It's fine. You didn't know so no harm done."

She looked up staring at something above my head and put her hand on her mouth and exclaimed, "Oh no! No! No! How's that possible!"

She looked at me with an extremely guilty look and exclaimed, "Hold on. I'll get the healing master right away. Hold on!"

Before I could ask what was wrong, she disappeared from my view leaving me wondering. I hadn't finished that thought when an excruciating pain shot through my shoulders. I cried out as the burning sensation slowly spread to the upper part of my arms. It felt like hundreds of glowing needles were making their way down to my arms. I couldn't do anything else than screaming the place down because of the torturing pain. It felt like ages until I heard footsteps and the sound of shouting echoing in a corridor.

A warm bronze voice shouted, "Why did you wake him up? Didn't you see that I've just started the next batch?"

The girl's voice was hoarse when she said, "I failed to notice that you have started the sequence. I'm so sorry."

The man said with a soothing voice, "Never mind. I've restarted the sequence; he will feel nothing within a few moments."

I wanted to say something, but suddenly I felt little drops of rain falling on my skin that took me by surprise and the burning changed into a dull bearable pain. I relaxed a bit and I again I thought I had the opportunity to say something but the darkness surrounded me completely.

****

I woke up with a start, and I opened my eyes hoping to

see the girl again. The sky was orange, and the grass looked dry as if it hadn't been watered for ages. I right wrist felt itchy, and I tried to lift my arm. I could tense my muscles, but I was too weak to lift my arm. The fact that I could move my fingers just a little felt strange. Unfortunately, my left arm seemed to be not there or at least I couldn't determine if I still had a left arm. Strangely enough I couldn't turn my head to have a look. I couldn't lift anything; neither my head nor my upper body. I felt like a rag doll lying on the grass.

I heard footsteps and within a few seconds the girl's face appeared in my vision. She wore a serious expression on her face as she said, "I want to apologise for what I've done to you. I seriously didn't know that another sequence had started."

I remembered the immense pain, and I winced a little. I said, "Yes, it was very painful."

Something was not right here because I couldn't get angry. A tear rolled down her cheek, and she whispered, "I'm so sorry."

I cleared my throat, and I said, "Don't cry. Please don't cry. You look much nicer when you don't cry."

She sniffed before saying "I've been so stupid."

I tried to smile, "Everyone can make a mistake. You're not stupid. I'll bet you won't make that mistake ever again."

She wiped the tear from her cheek and asked, "Bet? What is that?"

Her question was unsettling because I realised that I couldn't give her an explanation, and I had to rephrase the sentence. "I mean I'm sure you won't make that mistake again."

Again I had the feeling I wanted to say something but I couldn't put my finger on what. My body felt restless as if it wanted something else to happen, but I hadn't a clue what.

She shivered and said, "I didn't sleep for days."

I looked at her eyes, and I was surprised that I hadn't seen the dark lines under them before. I felt sorry for her, and I said, "I'm sorry, but I'm glad you're here now."

She blushed, and it looked like that she didn't know what to say.

My uneasiness was growing as well, and I tried to defuse the situation by asking, "Can I ask you a question?"

She smiled and said, "Of course, ask. But I can't promise if I'll answer it."

I couldn't put the real question in words, so I asked, "Do I still have two arms? I can't feel my left arm."

Her warm smile gave me the hope that everything would be fine soon. Her hand moved a strand of my hair away, and she said cheerfully, "Don't be silly! Of course, you have two arms. Have patience, it will be fine."

"Why can't I feel it?"

She frowned and shrugged her shoulders when she said, "I don't know. I'm not the healing master, but he assured me that you would recover just fine."

I sighed, and I said, "If you say so."

She sighed as well and then she suddenly asked out of the blue, "Do you still want to know my name?"

I was totally surprised by her question. I didn't understand why she suddenly wanted to tell me her name. It made me feel special, and I stammered, "If, if you don't mind telling me."

Her cheeks blushed a little when she said softly, "My name is Estrella."

Her name was beautiful; it had a real nice ring to it. I tried to remember my name but realised that I must be suffering from amnesia because I was unable to remember anything before the time I first saw Estrella. I decided not to mention that I couldn't remember my name, so I smiled, and I said genuinely, "Estrella. You have a beautiful name."

"Thank you," she said a little embarrassed.

She looked away momentarily, and when she next laid

her eyes on me, she whispered, "See you next time. Thanks for not being too upset."

I reassured her by saying, "I'm looking forward to our next meeting. Goodbye, Estrella."

At the moment she was gone I knew what I wanted to ask; why am I here? What happened to me?

I wanted answers, and I shouted, "Estrella!"

I felt my eyes getting droopy again, and I knew I was too late. But this time the darkness wasn't that scary anymore; the beautiful blue grey eyes of her were accompanying me to the abyss.

CHAPTER TWO.

The sky was purple and to my huge relief I noticed that I had regained the feeling in both of my arms. I was able to clench my fists, but it seemed that I couldn't lift my arms. It was as if they were restrained in a certain way. I couldn't move my head either, and I could clearly feel that something was keeping my whole body from moving. There were no straps, but it felt like that every part of my body was pinned to one place. If I didn't try to move, I couldn't feel the restraint at all, and it was as if I was lying freely on the grass.

I heard footsteps and looked forward to seeing Estrella again. "Hello, Estrella, nice of you to visit me again."

A woman appeared in my field of vision, and her stern expression made me feel very uncomfortable. I was shocked by her appearance. The shiny layer of powder made her face look puffy and gave her face an unnatural, even colour. Her lips looked too large for her face because they were painted in a fluorescent pink colour. Her eyes were done up with thick layers of metallic green eyeshadow, and her fake eyelashes were long. A drag queen would be extremely jealous because of the hideous amount of makeup she had used.

She huffed and said with an annoyed voice, "I can't believe she gave her name to this pathetic looking creature."

I was surprised to hear the healing master reply softly, "With all my respect Your Highest, he is practically the same as we are. His DNA is one-hundred-percent compatible with ours."

The idea of having sex with her made me shiver, and I noticed she had more or less the same reaction. She grunted, "He looks so ugly, so barbaric. I can't show him like that to anyone."

I had to bite my tongue not to make a sarcastic remark. This so-called "highest" woman looked hideous, and I didn't want to be her trophy to be paraded in front of her pompous friends. However, I knew I had to be careful because she might be a powerful person capable of eliminating me in an instant.

For the first time, the healing master appeared in my field of vision as well. I was not surprised to see him wearing an immaculate white jacket. His old wrinkly friendly face had a relaxing effect on me, and he asked, "How do you feel?"

I cleared my throat, and I said, "I feel fine. Thank you, healing master."

His smile met his eyes, and he said, "Good, I'm glad. Your body is responding very well to the treatment, and it seems it's adapting faster after every new batch."

The woman looked bored and while she inspected her hand, which was covered with huge kitsch rings, said, "When do you think he will be up to any activities?"

The healing master looked at her with a concerned expression on his face as he said, "Well, he needs about two more batches and after that the preparations of the regeneration can be started, Your Highest."

The woman sighed and asked, "How many cycles?"

"It depends on how long the healing process takes, Your Highest, but I would imagine at least fifteen cycles."

The woman moved closer to me, and I was shocked to realise she had the same blue grey eyes as Estrella. Her necklace was as pompous as her rings, and the huge diamond-like stone was dangling right in front of me when she sneered, "You are only alive because of her wish. Don't think you can use that for anything else. Do you understand?"

I blinked because I hadn't anticipated her sudden sneer. I was happy that I had kept my calm, and I said softly, "Yes Your Highest, I understand."

She looked at the healing master and murmured, "All right fix this creature and see if you find a way to speed it up. You're spending too much time on it."

He bowed a little when she walked away and said, "I'll do my best, Your Highest."

After I was certain she was gone, I asked, "Where is Estrella?"

He looked sad, "She isn't allowed to visit you anymore."

"Oh no, why not?"

"She made her mother cross."

I almost cried when I heard the last sentence, and I whispered, "Please don't tell me that this woman is her mother."

He sighed. "I'm afraid she is. Now, are you ready for the next batch?"

I wasn't ready for the next batch because I needed answers, and I said sternly, "No, I'm not ready."

His voice was very calm when he said, "Oh?"

"Why am I here?"

The healing master replied instantly, "Because Estrella brought you here."

"What are you doing to me?"

"Saving your life."

Damn! That was serious! Even it was not really what I wanted to hear, but it made me realise that his work was necessary.

I was starting to get tired of those short lived moments and as I looked him straight in his eyes I asked, "Why don't you do all the batches in a row without waking me up?"

He looked away at something I couldn't see when he said, "It can't be done like that. You need to recover from each batch. It will kill you if we give you them in one go. I have already tried to keep the number of times we wake you up to an absolute minimum."

I was shocked to hear that, and I asked him, "What are you doing that is so severe?"

"I'm afraid I don't have time to explain it right now. I've already started another batch, and you'll go to sleep in a few moments."

I was starting to get pissed off because I was not at all pleased with his evasive answers, and I practically shouted, "But, I want."

That was all I was able to yell before I felt the sudden rush going to my head. The choir of voices started to chant, and the darkness was inevitable.

****

The sky was bright red. It was too bright, and I closed my eyes trying to keep my eyes from being hurt. I heard footsteps reaching up to me, and I knew the steps were too heavy to be Estrella. I opened my eyes just enough to see the contour of the healing master and I felt strange but also quite at ease.

I knew I had shouted at him, but I had the feeling something was not quite right, and I asked, "How am I doing?"

His bronze voice was always pleasant to hear. "You're exceeding all expectations. Your recovery time has been reduced by seventy percent."

I was relieved, and smiling said, "Good, can you tone down the light a little? The red sky is too bright."

He sighed. "I was afraid that might happen."

His remark made my heart suddenly beat a lot faster. I knew it! "What is wrong, healing master?"

"Her Highest ordered us to speed up your healing process, and now you're suffering the consequences."

Oh shit! That bitch had caused me trouble! My heart was now beating like crazy, and I hardly dared to ask the question. "Am I going to die?"

The healing master laughed and said, "No, no. Don't worry. You're doing extremely well, but your vision has been affected by the treatment. It's a feedback system to give me an indication as to how the treatment has been received."

I sighed with relief, and I said, "So red means a little too much."

He huffed, "The amount administered would have killed a normal person but apparently your body can endure extremely high concentrations of this medicine."

Bloody hell! What was he using? I wondered what he was trying to say, and I sincerely hoped I would get a confirmation. My voice sounded feeble when I asked, "So you're done for now?"

Because of the bright red sky I couldn't really see the expression on his face but I could hear the uncertainty in his voice when he said, "For now, we are done but you need to recover from the treatment."

I was glad to hear that, and I said eagerly, "So no more blackouts from now."

He chuckled and waited for a few seconds before he revealed, "Not really. It is better to sleep off the after effects unless you want to be severely nauseous for two cycles. And trust me the next time, you wake up, will be quite revealing."

My heart sunk knowing I was going to face the darkness again I asked, "Can we just wait for a few hours?"

"Do you want to see Estrella again?"

Damn, I realised he got me by the balls, and I said,

"Yes, of course!"

"Then let me put you to sleep. I promise you'll see her the moment you wake up again."

Reluctantly I admitted to myself I had no other choice and the thought that I could see Estrella again was very exciting. I sighed, and I said, "All right, let's do it."

The healing master chuckled. "I knew you would go for that, but I must warn you; it will be a quite different experience when you wake up."

I still couldn't see his face because of the environment that was too bright and I asked, "What will be different?"

"Everything."

I wanted to ask more, but I already had the feeling that the sleeping drug was doing its work, and I sincerely hoped that the next time I fell asleep it would be without any drugs. The choir of voices was extremely loud before the darkness took me into a scary nothingness.

CHAPTER THREE.

I woke up with a start, and I instantly knew I was freed from the drug. My head was clear, but I still felt a bit woozy. I heard a soft humming and a regular ticking noise echoing in the small room. I still had my eyes closed because I wanted to take it easy. There wasn't much light in the room because I saw no light through my eyelids. My body felt weird as if I was lying in water because I couldn't feel I was touching any surface, and I was sure I was lying on my back. I carefully moved my index finger, and it felt funny as if I was stirring in a bowl of runny jelly. When I tried to lift my arm, it took a huge effort but eventually I felt my skin getting cold when it reached the surface. Now I was sure my body was floating in a basin filled with warm jelly.

I opened my eyes.

I closed them again.

I opened them again to be sure that it didn't make any difference, but then I saw a little red light in the corner of my eye. The room was just totally dark except for the little red light. I tried to turn my face towards the light, but I noticed that my head was strapped in. Presumably to preventing me from slipping down into the jelly.

The healing master was right: it was completely different.

It was quite sobering to find yourself floating in a basin full of warm jelly. I'm not sure what kind of drugs the healing master had used to keep me at bay, but it had some serious hallucinatory powers!

I was not sure what to do.

I could shout to see if someone came to my assistance or just wait until they came and checked on me. I decided to wait and use the time to contemplate what had happened to me. I was startled to realise that this was the first time that I had been alone and not under the influence of drugs.

I wanted to know what the purpose of the regeneration ceremony was, and of course, what they had done to me.

Why this jelly basin?

How long have I been here?

Where was here?

Why couldn't I remember my life before I met Estrella and why did I have the feeling that I had led a completely different life previously?

It troubled me that I sensed that I had seen Estrella before and was unable to remember where.

The door opened, and a woman dressed in a slim fitting white suit entered the room. She was tall and as she moved her well-toned body graciously to a panel she cheerfully said, "Good morning, a splendid day to get you out of your support unit."

The room lights started to glow softly and for the first time I saw I was in a small room. Except for the huge basin I was floating in there was nothing else.

The nurse was stunningly beautiful. Her hair was done up in a bun, and her almond shaped brown eyes made her round face look magical. Her bright red lips turned into a smile when she saw me look totally flabbergasted. She chuckled and said, "I think you need a proper bath."

Not really understanding what she was going to do I

said, "Well, it seems I'm in a bath already."

She giggled and walked to me and checked my eyes with a little flashlight. She behaved like the healing master when she asked, "How do you feel? Do you have a headache?"

"I feel a little strange, but I don't have a headache."

"Good. Now *this* is going to feel a bit strange."

She reached above me, and I heard a little beep. At that moment, I felt something tucking at my privates but before it started to feel uncomfortable, it was over. I realised that I had tubes in me which prevented me from fouling the jelly. I was glad that she didn't do that by hand. It would have been very uncomfortable, and it made me blush just thinking about it.

She noticed that my cheeks were red and asked as if that was normal for me, "No pain?"

My voice was suddenly a bit hoarse, "No, no pain."

Her smile was back again, and she said, "Perfect. I'm going to loosen the restraints on your head. I know this will feel weird but please try and keep your head as still and straight as possible. After that, the jelly will be pumped out of the basin, which can be a bit uncomfortable but I'll get you out of there as quick as possible."

I knew that my muscles were weak, but I still had some strength, however, was not certain that I would be able to stand. I asked, "What can I do to help?"

"Act like a dolly."

"You mean like a forgotten string puppet that is lying in a corner looking sad because the strings are tangled into a knot?"

Her laugh was genuine. "Yes, something like that."

I murmured, "Piece of cake."

She smiled at me for a moment before murmuring, "Ready?"

"When you are."

"Right, here it goes."

A humming noise made the basin tremble a bit and

within a few moments I felt that a part of my chest was exposed to the air. The level of the jelly dropped with a fast pace, and I started to notice small surfaces that were supporting my body. The more jelly was pumped out; the more weight was pressed on the small surfaces. It felt uncomfortable, and I had a vague idea how it must feel when you were lying on a bed of nails.

At the moment it became unbearable, the nurse said with a smile, "Hugging time."

She quickly took my arms and put them on her shoulders one on each side of her neck. Then suddenly the whole basin turned towards her, and I felt myself falling onto her body. With one gracious movement, she lifted me up against her body while she had one arm under my bottom.

My head rested against her neck, and I smelled her delicate perfume. It was something precious: it was the first nice experience that was real.

I still felt like a rag doll, but I liked the feeling of helplessness. The delicate sensation of lying against her warm and soft body was marvellous.

She said with a little strain in her voice, "That went smoothly. Now the fun part will begin."

I couldn't resist saying, "This is fun already. Can't wait to find out what you're planning to do with me."

While she was carrying me through a door, she said, "Haha, you'll see. There will be a few surprises."

I liked our daring conversation a lot, and I said excited, "Bring it on."

She chuckled as we entered a much warmer room, and I heard water plunging into the water.

She turned around slowly to show me where we were, and she said, "Bathing time. Let's make you a bit more human again."

I couldn't believe my eyes!

The room consisted of a huge bath that was constantly filled by a waterfall. At the end of the room was a small stream where the excess water flowed away. The nurse walked down the steps into the bath, and I was surprised by how warm the water was. I released a sigh of contentment; I enjoyed the gentle flow of the warm water caressing my body.

She put me down on a spongy surface which completely supported my body and asked, "What shall we do first? Wash your hair, wash your body or shave your beard?"

I moved my hand to my chin, and I was shocked to discover I had a beard of at least four inches long. I couldn't recall I had ever had a beard before, and I didn't like the feeling of it at all. I replied resolutely, "Beard first."

She clapped her hands as her eyes twinkled. "Oh great! It has been ages since I have shaved a man."

I raised my eyebrow and asked, "Err, you'll be careful now would you?"

Her nearly demonic smile made me feel like a teenage boy that had asked a drop dead gorgeous woman a really stupid question. She purred, "I know how to handle shaving gear on delicate surfaces."

Her response took a while to sink in, and when it finally dawned on me, my scarlet red face made her giggle.

Her sultry voice hardly calmed me down when she said, "Relax and enjoy, this is one of the few times it's done for you."

She was right, though: it's one of the daily routines that I apparently hadn't done for quite a while.

After she had cut off the long hairs, she started to massage the shaving cream into the stubbles with her soft fingers. When the hairs on my chin were soft enough, she removed my beard with precise movements using an extremely sharp razor knife.

Her soft fingers traced the bare skin of my face and she said, "Right, what do you want now?"

I liked her massaging skills, and I said, "I think we should keep your hands above water for the moment. So can you wash my hair?"

"Hmmm, you want to save the real fun for last?"

Her answer made me smile, and I said with a low voice, "Everything that you do is nice."

****

I was lying face down on a table while the nurse was massaging my legs with her strong hands. It had been quite an interesting adventure, and I felt squeaky clean all over. I was pleased that she was a very experienced nurse who knew how to wash a man. My hair was in a ponytail, and she convinced me it looked really good on me. It was one of those strange situations where I had to make a decision on the spot.

She commanded me in her sensual voice while washing my body, and it was an experience I would never forget.

The nurse patted on my legs and said, "Right, next adventure. The power suit."

She turned me on my back again, and I saw she was still wearing the wet and tight-fitting suit that clung to her like a second skin. For the first time, I noticed her breasts, and I thought they were in perfect proportion with her body. I didn't have more time to admire her body because she lifted me from the table as if I were weightless.

My neck muscles were sore from trying to keep my head upright, and I was pleased when the nurse put me on a weird chair that supported my head as well.

Then I noticed that the form of the chair completely supported my body. The nurse kneeled down and strapped my feet into a kind of shoes which were connected to the legs of the chair.

Before I had a chance to object, my whole body was strapped into this remarkable chair. Even my head was completely secured.

She walked around me while she was double checking the straps, and she said, "That's a wrap!"

I snickered and said trying to show off my word game, "Too bad you can't eat me."

Her face turned into a cunning smirk, as she moved her beautiful mouth closer to my ear saying with the most seductive voice I had ever heard, "Say "Menu" out loud."

I hesitated, and I looked surprised at her. I must have misunderstood her, and I asked, "What?"

Moving close and with her finger on her lips she said "You want to know what's on the menu. So say, "Menu"."

As she moved away a little, I obediently said, "Menu."

A small display appeared at eye level with a list of options that are all grey except "Activate". I was flabbergasted how this display appeared in front of my eye from nowhere and how sharp the text items were.

With a soft voice, because I was afraid that it would react immediately upon hearing my voice,

"You want me to say that word?"

There was a twinkle in her eye when she replied, "Yes, don't worry nothing will happen."

I realised I was behaving like an anxious man, so I decided to counter that by saying firmly, "Activate."

I heard a little beep, and it sounded like that several little motors were spinning up to a high pitched tone.

She checked a few places at the chair and said with a cheery voice, "Good. All green, now say, "stand"."

Again I was not sure of myself but I trusted my lovely nurse and I complied resolutely. As soon as I had said the word the chair changed in form and before I had fathomed what happened I was standing straight up. I felt light headed by the sudden movement that caused my blood to leave my sore head.

Again the nurse walked around me, and when she stood in front of me, she said, "They have done a good job. It fits perfectly. Right, I'm done. Except for one little thing."

I raised my eyebrows, and a mesmerising smile appeared on her pretty face. She brought her hand to the top of her suit and moved it slowly down. The flaps of her suit fell sideways revealing her still wet bra that was practically see-through. Her soft skin shined like silk, and her bra created a wonderful cleavage between her full breasts.

Here I was, standing completely strapped in, looking at a beautiful woman who was undressing herself slowly. Her cunning smile and her teasing way of undressing made my heart beat faster causing extra blood to flow to my groin.

She removed her bra, and her firm breasts nearly defied gravity making them look even more magnificent. I stared at her breathtakingly beautiful pink nipples that were protruding from perfect round and just little lighter areolas.

I didn't know what to say!

My cheeks were extremely hot, and I felt my member pushing hard against the soft fabric. I wondered why she was undressing like that in front of me until I saw her staring at my groin with great interest. I hated that I was stuck in this so-called power suit, and I felt utterly powerless and completely vulnerable; unable to hide my aroused state.

She licked her lips and said with a husky voice, "I'm glad that the healing master didn't forget that part."

She walked to the door with her suit still halfway off, and her breasts bounced a little with each step she took. She was so beautiful, and I was very disappointed she was leaving me alone just like that.

Before she left the room, she turned her head and said while winking at me, "It was a pleasure to fix you up. See you later, the healing master will help you connect with your power suit."

I couldn't believe what just happened to me. Her little show left me with a throbbing member, and I was going to face the healing master like this. I desperately needed to try to get myself calmed down, but her beautiful body was still engraved in my retina.

I needed to cool down!

What if this highest lady saw me like this? Recalling that moment when the healing master told us we were one-hundred-percent compatible instantly helped me to cool down my aroused state. With a huge sigh of relief, I noticed that my cock was more or less flaccid again.

Hearing footsteps in the hall, I was glad I didn't have time to think about the super-hot nurse anymore.

The healing master entered the room and said with a huge smile, "Ah, good. The nurse helped you out as agreed."

I chuckled, and I said, "Yes, she minutely checked every part of my body." I felt a small blush appearing on my face when I remembered the manner in which she had aroused me.

He walked around me touching the suit at several places and said, "Excellent. Now let's link you up with the power suit."

I had no idea what that implied, but I wanted to talk first about what had happened to me. I cleared my throat, and I said, "Actually, I want to ask you a few questions before you link me up."

He walked to a panel and asked nearly absent minded, "What is it you want to know?"

I looked at the screen the healing master was looking at, and I said, "I want to know what happened to me. Why did I need so many treatments?"

While he was flipping a few small switches, he said, "You were struck by lightning that destroyed most of your nerve system."

I stammered, "I, I survived a lightning strike?"

He turned his face and said proudly, "Yes, it was quite a challenge to rebuild all your nerves. First we removed the burned ones, and then we replaced them with a nerve solution of a Garntuoa."

I looked at him while my mouth had dropped open.

He continued ignoring my distress, "Garntuoa nerves

are capable of regenerating provided the sleeve of the nerve is more or less intact. In your case, ninety-nine point nine percent of your nerve sleeves were intact except at the point of entry. Luckily there was only one major nerve that I could replace easily together with the damaged tissue."

I asked, "Does that mean I have a complete new nerve system in my body?"

"Yes, you have."

I tried to comprehend the consequences, and I asked, "How long did the healing process take?"

The healing master was entering some numbers on a screen while he said, "It took us four hundred cycles, which is roughly a year on your planet."

I was shocked.

A whole year! A whole bloody year wasted!

But I was not surprised when he unintentionally confirmed that I was on a different planet, and it brought more peace of mind than I thought it would. I was still wondering what had happened to my memory, and I asked, "I'm missing parts of my memory is that a side effect of this treatment?"

He turned around and looked straight at me, "Your memory loss is due in part to the treatment. We needed to be sure that your history was safeguarded, so we removed it and stored it in a safe place."

I hadn't suspected that memories had been deliberately removed, and starting to get annoyed I demanded to know why they had done that.

His expression on his face was placid when he said, "It is by law that non-Youriens come immaculately to our world. Try to turn your head towards me."

I was truly taken aback by what he just had said, and it took a long moment for his command to sink in.

I carefully tried to move my head towards the panel the healing master was working at. At first it didn't want to cooperate but after a second or two I managed to turn my head. I asked, "You mean my history as in how I had lived my life on my planet has been removed from my memory and stored somewhere safe."

"Yes, that is a way to sum it up. Hmmm interesting," he mumbled, "The suit is geared to normal nerve activities and not to the activity levels of Garntuoa nerves. Move your fingers on your right hand by making a fist and open up again and do that for several times."

As I was closing and opening my fist, I heard a female voice saying in my ear, "Calibrating."

While I felt, my weak muscles were getting tired quickly from the simple exercise until a little beep sounded, and a voice said, "Calibration complete."

The next thing I knew I was collapsing like jelly, and I had the presence of mind to practically shout the command, "Stand!"

The speed that the power suit was responding to my command was incredibly fast, and the suit made even a little jump before it stood.

The healing master laughed when I was standing there like a solid sculpture. He said, "Let's try this again."

CHAPTER FOUR.

It was a weird feeling walking again, but I was able to follow the healing master quite easily.

It took us four attempts before the suit started responding correctly to my body and after that it took me about ten minutes before I was able to keep my poise again. The power suit had been specifically designed to help me move my muscles and at the moment it was set to provide eighty percent support.

We walked for a while through different corridors before coming to a halt in a large hall. He said, "Wait here. If you feel uncertain about standing you can try walking in little circles."

I answered, "I'll do my best to keep out of trouble."

He grinned and walked through a door leaving me alone.

I still had trouble maintaining my balance, and I decided to take a look at the remarkable works of art which adorned the walls. This hall was clearly meant for receiving guests.

One painting, in particular, captured my imagination, and I wondered briefly about the artist. I took a closer look, trying to see if there were any identifying marks.

Unfortunately, there was nothing that connected it to the artist.

I heard a rustle of clothes, and spinning around, I was pleased to see that it was Estrella. Her grey-blue eyes widened when she saw me and her cheeks flushed as she said, "You look much better without a beard."

She looked even more beautiful than I could remember. I chuckled, and I said, "Thanks, I didn't know I had grown one."

She said remorsefully, "I'm sorry I couldn't be there the last few times."

"Don't be Estrella. It wasn't your fault."

Her eyes became glassy, and she whispered, "My mother doesn't like you."

I sighed. "I know. Do you know why?"

She took my hand and said softly, "It seems you're not representative enough."

I raised my eyebrows.

She giggled. "I think you're fun. I think she doesn't understand your sophisticated humour."

At the very moment, I opened my mouth to make a funny remark I heard a harsh voice shouting, "Estrella!"

Turning too quickly, I lost my balance causing me to tumble forward on my hands and knees. My embarrassment was complete when I felt the blood rushing to my face as Estrella pulled me back to my feet. I was totally taken aback at how strong she was and within a few moments I was on my feet again facing her mother with a crushed dignity.

I managed to bow, and I said subdued, "Your Highest."

As she looked me up and down, she said, "You look a bit better without the beard. I've heard you just got out of your basin?"

Her compliment gave me a little more confidence to answer her question without a stammer. "Yes, Your Highest, I still need to get used to this power suit."

She turned her attention to Estrella and said, "You have twenty-five cycles to make up your mind and prove your choice is valid."

Estrella's face brightened as she bowed to her mother and murmured softly, "We will be ready within the time, mother."

Her mother harrumphed, "Many others have been before you, and they all have failed. Why should this time be different?"

Her resolute answer made me shiver, "Because we will succeed, mother."

When Estrella's mother turned to me again, I noticed that her face didn't have any makeup, and she looked much nicer. She even managed to smile a bit when she said, "My daughter believes you can defeat history. I'm looking forward to the regeneration ceremony."

The only thing I could do was bow again, and I said, "I'll try not to disappoint you and Estrella, Your Highest."

"You're a quick learner, so I'm willing to give you the benefit of the doubt."

I was taken aback by her response, and I bowed deeply nearly losing my balance again and I said sincerely, "Thank you, Your Highest."

She turned and walked away with sturdy steps.

When I gazed up to meet Estrella's eyes, I knew I was stuck in a dangerous game. I was flabbergasted by what had just happened. Certain that I had been lured into something I wanted nothing to do with. What the hell had she just arranged with her mother?

She said with a tremble in her voice, "We need to talk."

I couldn't hide my sarcasm in my voice when I said, "You're kidding me."

She shrivelled; shocked by the venom in my voice.

"It's not what you think."

Oh right! What a stupid answer, as if I can't think for myself!

I scoffed, "Oh really? Are you telling me that you didn't

intend to show me off? You're as bad as your mother."

Her mouth opened and shut again, her eyes narrowing. Her face was flushed with embarrassment, or maybe it was fury and her lips were formed in a thin line.

I knew that I had overreacted, but I didn't care about it anymore, and I exclaimed, "Have you ever thought about to asking me first *before* you promise anything to your mom?"

A solitary tear ran down her cheek as she growled, "Well, I'm sorry. I think it's best you use your right to go back to your pathetic little planet if you are well enough."

She turned around and rushed away without glancing back at me at all. I was dumbstruck by her heated reaction that was way over the top. I guessed she had inherited the bad temper from her mother, and I doubted if I wanted to be part of it all.

I felt my anger growing, and I needed to get out of this retarded place. I started to march angrily away from the hall into one of the many corridors without paying attention. I was truly disappointed by the unrealistic decisions forced on me by Estrella. I thought she liked me, but now she wanted me to be the hero of the century.

Hell!

I couldn't even walk around normally without this weird power suit.

****

I had been going around in circles for quite a while before I finally managed to find the room where my basin was.

I looked at the empty basin with a funny feeling in my stomach knowing that I had been in that metal case for at least a year. I was wondering how many times Estrella had been here just looking at me.

Why did she have so much interest in me?

Why did I think about her again?

What had I done?

Why was I so special?

Why did she set me up for this special regeneration ceremony?

I recognised the footsteps of the healing master, and when he entered the room he said with a joyful voice, "Ah, there you are! We've been looking for you."

The enthusiastic tone in his voice softened my mood considerably, and I smiled. "I was lost until I finally found the room."

"Hmmm, yes you've been here for a long time in this old rusty barrel. It's time for something more luxurious. Let me show you your new quarters and after that I would like you to come and have something to eat."

The word "eat" instantly triggered a loud rumble in my stomach, and we both started to laugh. He said, "Aha, Pavlov!"

I couldn't believe what he just had said, and I asked, "I'm sorry what did you just say?"

He saw my surprised expression and he said with some pride in his eyes, "I have been studying your world for a while now, and I think it's fascinating how you are developing. I think the Pavlov study is very interesting."

"Why did you study our science?"

"Because of you of course. I wanted to know more about your world and since you've been with us for more than four hundred cycles I had plenty of time."

I slowly nodded my head as if I was trying to comprehend the huge amount he must have studied to come across the theory of Pavlov.

****

My food consisted of some water and a cocktail of mashed up vegetables and fruits. I felt like a toddler who was not used to eating grown up food. The healing master assured me that after a few days my stomach would be able to deal with solid food again. It made it easy to take some tubes filled with nutritious food with me, which looks like toothpaste tubes. I tried a little, and the paste tasted like an extremely sweet banana and orange smoothie. The healing master said that one tube had enough nutrition to last for two days without anything else to eat.

It was weird eating the mashed up dinner, but I was more disturbed by the fact that I couldn't remember what I liked to eat before I was struck by lightning and kidnapped by aliens! I could vaguely remember Estrella pleading with the healing master to fix me up, but anything before that was gone.

How was I able to remember snippets of information about scientists like Pavlov? Their skill at removing your personal memories was remarkable, but how was I still able to remember details of my education?

****

Totally exhausted I lay down on my bed in my power suit because my muscles were too weak to be able to be in bed without it. It had been an eventful day, and I remembered it with mixed emotions. Coming out the "old barrel" and being groomed by an utterly hot sexy nurse. Thinking back to the moment she showed her amazing body made my desire for her flair up again. The awkward moment she left me with my hard-on and her naughty wink kept me wide awake.

I still couldn't understand how the quarrel I had with Estrella had escalated so badly.

My mind kept on racing around trying to process all the new information, and I was torn in two: on one hand I wanted to stay and the other I wanted to go back to my homeland.

But there was another dilemma: I had no idea who I was and what I did at home. Was it better? Would I like my life back there? Was I even the same person anymore since my nerves had been blended with the Garntuoa?

I was tossing around in my bed which was awkward because the power suit felt clunky, and I couldn't find a position to lay comfortable. I wanted to be out of the suit as soon as possible, and I decided to start with a rigorous training program as from tomorrow. The healing master had showed me during our meal, the possibilities of the power suit that were very impressive.

I loved the fact that it had a complete navigation system including maps of the whole planet. I was looking forward to hiking in the countryside. It seemed that the planet's climate was very pleasant and if I stayed within a hundred miles of the county, the risk of encountering dangerous animals was extremely small.

I wanted to gain my normal capabilities as soon as possible and then decide what I was going to do. Although right now, I was so fed up that I would leave this strange planet straight away if I could.

Finally, after I had set some goals, I felt a bit more relaxed, and I fell asleep.

****

It took me a few moments after opening my eyes to realise where I was, and I was pleased I had woken up at my own pace. I felt fresh for the first time in ages.

My new place had a window that looked out onto a beautifully maintained garden, and I could see it was a bright sunny day. It was the perfect moment to discover the place.

After I had eaten, I began walking along one of the roads. The weather was nice: the temperature was pleasant and the light breeze was refreshing. I began jogging and to my surprise it felt nice to let the muscles work a little harder.

It was all a little too easy, and I turned the support of

the suit down to seventy-five percent. The extra strain on my muscles gave me a satisfying feeling.

The roads I was walking on were not used anymore, but they looked as if they were new. I wondered if they were self-maintaining, something I vowed to ask the healing master later.

The fresh air and being surrounded by amazingly interesting nature made me feel completely at ease. I truly enjoyed my first day out in the open.

After I had been jogging for a while, I began to feel a little sweaty, and I was startled by a beep from my power suit. I had forgotten that I had set myself a restriction for the first time, and my power suit just had indicated that I had to turn around because I was halfway through my trip. I knew now already that I was going to miss the power suit when I was fit enough to be without it.

As soon as the complex came into sight, I decided to speed up so that I was semi-running. I was flabbergasted that I could run with hardly any effort at all. It was as if my body was telling me that it wanted much more like this.

The sweat was running down my face after I had run the last mile as fast as I could and when I returned to my quarters a nurse was waiting for me. She was not as stunning as the previous nurse, but her smile disarmed me completely.

Her voice was soft and sounded pleasant to my ear when she said, "Good morning. I'm nurse Layly. Do you want to have a bath?"

It was funny that she told me her name as if it was a normal thing to do, and it made me aware that I couldn't remember my name.

I was still heavily out of breath and while I was trying to get enough air to speak I was pondering what to do. I made a decision on the spot that it was time to choose a *new* name. I was not really bothered that I didn't know my real name, and I had the feeling that I had become another person anyway. As I mulled over potential names

"Xander" popped into my mind. I was content with the way it sounded, and I decided that I shouldn't dither about it any longer.

I replied while still panting a bit, "Yes, Layly I think I would like to have a bath. Please call me Xander."

Her face lit up, and she giggled nervously. "Xander, a beautiful name. Would you follow me?"

I thought I would get used to it, but I still would like to be able to wash myself. Luckily Layly didn't seem remotely interested in me sexually and was happy to talk,

She told me that she would be my personal assistant for the rest of my stay as long as I needed it.

I was grateful that the fabric inner lining of the power suit was exchangeable because the thought of having to get back into a sweaty power suit filled me with dread.

Freshly washed and in a crisp looking power suit I went to the dining hall to have breakfast. I was starving.

CHAPTER FIVE.

I began to get into a routine where I was discovering the surroundings of the county in the morning while I was training my body. After the bathing session with nurse Layly, I usually lay down to have a short sleep. Then I had lunch mostly accompanied by the healing master who checked my physical being.

In the afternoon, I completed another intense training session and after dinner I was too tired to do anything else but sleep.

I would have been bored to death if I followed the same route every time I went out. Other than the healing master and Layly, I didn't have many people to talk to. I felt isolated, and it was almost as if I had done something wrong. Whenever I tried discussing it with Layly she was deliberately evasive.

On day five my muscles were already strong enough to sleep without the power suit. Falling asleep with the blanket pressed against your body was difficult, but I was glad to be free from the encapsulated hard shell of the power suit.

The only thing that bothered me a little was the fact I never had any serious discomfort of aching muscles because I could just dull the pain somehow. I was sure that my Garntuoa nerves had a huge influence on the painless and quick development of my muscles. In the following days, I experimented a little more, and I found out I could numb the pain. I bit on my finger until it was painful, and then I concentrated on the painful place until the pain was nearly gone.

As the days passed by I was pleased, I had a target, and it looked like that it would only be a matter of a few days before I was freed from the suit.

Every time I thought about Estrella and our fight, I became angry and usually started to run faster in an attempt to run away from the agony. I was more determined than ever to get into the best, possible shape so that I could get the hell out of here. I didn't understand why I was still was so upset about it. Every time I remembered her pretty face my stomach knotted and remained that way until I had managed to focus completely on something else. Running as fast as I could seemed like a good solution.

As I got stronger my hunger for heavier training grew by the day, and I found myself change the power suit support to a negative number. I was amazed that you could change to a negative number, and there was no limit because I accidentally changed the setting to minus five hundred which resulted in me not being able to move my body at all.

This was the first time that I noticed that the suit was changing in size to accommodate the growth of my muscles. It was the beginning of the third week when I also had heard that it would take at least another twenty days, or cycles before I could be returned to my own planet.

I was very upset that I had to wait such a long time!

****

After a restless night during which I had come to terms with the fact that it was going to be a while before I was able to leave this planet, I decided to expand my training sessions to whole days. The less time that I spent in the city, the better. It was the first time that I took food for lunch with me for the longer trip that included a climb up a small mountain. The healing master had warned me to change the setting of the power suit that would protect me if I were to fall.

The first part of the journey was familiar and had two straight roads that I used to run. With my new nerves, I was able to run faster than ever before and every time I increased my speed by moving my muscles faster. It was as if I could change my perception of time: everything seemed to go slower when I was running that fast.

I looked at the map that because I was in new territory, I had opened on the display of the power suit. There was a red line on the map which indicated the border of the city's county. As I neared, the female voice of the power suit said, "Warning, you are about to leave the protection zone. Leaving the protection zone is at your own risk."

I knew that there was a chance of bumping into some wildlife but figured that most of it would be more afraid of me than I would be of them.

After fifteen minutes going at a steady pace, it was clear I had left the zone because the road was not as pristine as before. The vegetation that was grew over the path caused me to stumble.

The landscape changed quickly into a rough but amazing hilly scene with large trees, and the road was nothing more than an indication on my navigation system. It was hard work keeping up the speed as the rough and coarse surface was starting to become treacherous. I stopped for a while to catch my breath, and while I was looking around the power suit gave me a strange message, "Warning! Please be aware that the battery reserves are down to forty-five percent."

It was the first time that I had seen that message, and I was surprised that the suit could run out of energy. I dismissed the warning because I hadn't ever charged the suit, and I assumed that it would last at least a few more hours.

Feeling hungry, I paused to eat. Even though I loved the untouched nature out in the wilderness, I knew that it was time to return to the city. The roughness had its charm, and I felt really at ease.

As I was getting into a more leisurely running tempo, I caught a glimpse of an animal on my left that was easily keeping up with me. The dark brown furry animal was as big as a Saint Bernard, but it was a mix of a big cat and a dog. It was about fifty feet away running with me on a parallel route. I was wondering why it was following me until it suddenly disappeared. I was still busy thinking why it had disappeared when I saw it standing in front of me.

It was about thirty feet in front of me with its teeth bared growling a low rumbling noise. I knew that it would have no difficulty crushing my neck if it chose to; the row of sharp teeth looked like they could cut steel. I knew that my power suit would partially protect me and the only way out of this situation was to call the creatures bluff. That was my only hope of reaching the city border again.

I pumped my lungs full of air hoping that my little plan would work. I jumped up and down and started waving my arms, trying to make myself appear as big as possible, before shouting loud, "Move little beast, move!"

I accelerated, running straight at it, relieved as I saw the confusion in its eyes. The instincts of the animal took over and to my huge relief it started to run away.

I kept on running, and I didn't dare to look back. I slowed down my insane pace when I saw that the city's county border wasn't far anymore. I was so happy when I crossed the border that I didn't notice the red bar in the display of the power suit. When I slowed down to a normal walk the power suit's voice announced quite unexpectedly, "Battery reserve down to a dangerous level. Shutting down the interface. Would you like to initiate the emergency signal?"

I didn't understand what had happened, but I said, "Yes."

The suit responded, "Sending emergency signal and the locator transmitter is enabled."

I wanted to sit down to let my muscles rest, but nothing happened. I was stuck in a power suit that had ground to a complete halt!

I was shocked that I couldn't move at all! I thought I was strong enough to overcome the motors in the power suit, but here I was trapped in a solid shell with no chance of getting out without help!

Then fear gripped me. Where the hell had the wild animal gone?

I began stressing when I heard some rustling but was unable to move my head to see where it was.

The panting and sniffing was very close to me, and I kept my breathing as shallow as possible. I felt something pushing against my leg and then I saw the cat nuzzling its head against me while it was slowly walking around. I guessed the cat liked it because it started to purr so loud that I felt my power suit vibrating. I couldn't believe that this huge cat had changed into a loving animal, and I kept my breathing very slow while my heart pounded loudly in my throat.

The cat changed its purring into a whimpering sound, and I suddenly felt something else stroking my leg. It felt like a long slow lick from a big warm tongue.

It was licking my leg!

I felt the long strokes starting from my shin up to my knee, and the fabric of my trousers was slowly getting wet. The warm tongue kept on rasping against my now soaking wet leg, and it seemed that its persisting licking had an effect on my trousers.

I felt that the fabric was starting to get thinner, and the

animal licking was getting more passionate as if it knew it was getting closer to a nice snack.

The whining sound of the animal was getting louder, and suddenly I heard a loud clanging sound as if something had hit the power suit. I gasped when I heard the fabric tear, and a rough wet tongue touched my skin.

Strangely enough the warm tongue felt somewhat pleasant but after a few licks my skin started to hurt because of the constant scraping of the rough tongue. I knew sooner or later my skin would break, and my raw flesh would turn this cat wild.

What a way to die! Strapped into a dead power suit and unable to move at all.

I feverishly thought about what I should do, and I looked at the menu of the power suit. Unfortunately the option "activate" was still grey, I had hoped that the battery would have regained some energy.

I had to say the word "menu" out loud, and I realised too late that the animal would have heard that as well.

Two angry bright yellow eyes were staring at me, and it started to growl softly while it was baring its sharp teeth.

I was now top of its menu.

It slowly moved back a bit and crouched down to tighten its muscles ready to jump. Like a cat, it started to wiggle its hips all the while hissing softly.

I knew that the end of my life was near, and I shouted as loud as I could, "Move away stupid cat! MOVE!"

It had hardly any effect, and it postponed the inevitable attack just for a few moments. I closed my eyes trying not to think about how much I would suffer. Suddenly Estrella's nice face appeared in my mind, and I felt really sad that I never had the chance to make it up with her. Now I was going to be lunch for a ferocious cat.

This was the end.

I cursed softly that it would take longer to die because of the protection of the power suit.

The seconds were ticking away, and my heart was

pounding in my throat waiting for it to happen.

The growling had stopped.

This was it!

Any moment now!

I held my breath braced for the impact, but nothing happened!

Carefully opening my eyes, and I saw the cat looking away from me as if it was listening to something.

I didn't know what the cat had heard, but it had its full attention.

Then I heard a low humming noise which sounded like a man made machine.

Were they coming to get me?

The cat looked at me and then at the direction of the sound which was becoming louder with each passing second.

Then it looked back to me, and it was clear it decided to attack me anyway. It crouched down readying itself to jump in my face. The cat wiggled its hips and I saw the tension building in its muscles.

No!

Not again!

I didn't know what I had done to deserve such a horrific death. I pinched my eyes closed, not wanting to see the moment it launched itself at me.

It growled, and I was sent flying by the weight of the animal. I braced myself for the sharp teeth to rip off my face. However, the animal was limp.

A strong smell of scorched hair filled my nose, and when I opened my eyes, I looked straight at a gaping wound in the neck of the cat. Something extremely hot had punctured a deep hole in the neck of the animal! I couldn't believe it first, but I slowly began to understand that the creature had been killed.

Meanwhile, the low humming had stopped, and I heard footsteps hurrying towards me.

A male voice called out enthusiastically, "That was

close! What a beautiful shot, nurse Ellonary."

While the man was standing next to me, I recognised the sultry voice of the nurse, who had helped me out of the basin. "Thanks, I couldn't allow the Anix to hurt my lovely Xander. Could I?"

I thought I had died and gone to heaven.

I had been saved by the hottest nurse of the city who also happened to have an incredibly sensual name: Ellonary.

The man looked amused and said, "Hi Xander. You can count yourself very lucky that Ellonary is a skilled hunter."

I was extremely relieved, and I joked, "Yes, I felt like I was a sitting duck here for quite a while."

Based on the strange expression on his face I said, "Never mind, it is a silly joke."

Ellonary stood next to the man with a huge grin on her face and said, "Hi, how nice to bring such a large Anix to town."

The way she was looking at me made my heart beat faster, and I said trying to be as nonchalant as possible, "Yes, it liked me, so it followed me all the way here."

Her almond eyes grew bigger, and she asked, "You have been with the Anix since your suit started to send the emergency signal?"

"Yes, I survived because I couldn't move."

She exclaimed, "That is truly amazing!"

I smiled but the dead weight of the animal was starting to get uncomfortable, and I said, "Yes. But uh, would you be so kind to pull this uh, Anix off me because it is starting to feel quite heavy."

They instantly pulled the carcass off my body, and I was glad that I could breathe a lot easier after I was liberated.

The man said authoritatively, "We need to get the Anix away from here before it attracts other unwanted guests."

While Ellonary began unstrapping me from the power

suit she suggested, "Why don't you bring the Anix to the research centre."

He replied, "Yes good plan, but I can't take you all."

My guess that he was the pilot had now been confirmed. However, I was surprised that he wasn't wearing a special aviation suit.

Ellonary looked at me and asked, "Would you mind staying the night here with me?"

She had finished unstrapping me, and she traced her finger down my chest muscles that I unintentionally flexed. I saw a little twinkle in her eyes, and I knew she was more than surprised by how my muscles had developed. But even with her shooting skills I wasn't up to encountering more wildlife tonight. "Will it be safe? I mean, what if another Anix decides to visit?"

She looked at the pilot, "Do you have a dome at the hover?"

He raised his eyebrow, "You should know by now that it is part of the standard equipment."

Her eyes exuded a raw sexual desire, and she said as she patted my chest, "We will be safe, and your power suit can be charged overnight. So what do you think?"

I knew for sure that she had other plans than just sleep, and I definitely wouldn't mind being part of it. I got very excited by the idea, and I answered with a smirk, "Sounds like a perfect plan."

Her smile was mesmerising, and she purred, "Great! Let's get you out the suit so you can help us setting things up."

The pilot chuckled and said, "Alright, I'll get the dome and the charger."

It was a liberating feeling when Ellonary undid the last strap. I was a little rigid from being in the same position for such a long period, but it was gone after I helped her carrying the Anix to the hover.

The hover looked like a helicopter without the rotors, and I was wondering how it was able to fly. The pilot came out carrying a large transparent sack that was big enough to fit the Anix.

With some effort, we managed to get the animal packed into the sack ready for the trip, and we heaved the cat into the hover.

The pilot said, "Well I have another grand story to tell the boys at home."

I snickered a bit, and I said, "Tell them that an Anix likes to lick you first before it starts to nibble on your nose."

Ellonary shivers and said, "I'm so glad I had it at the first time."

The pilot shook my hand and said, "I guess I'll see you somewhere in the city."

Ellonary gave the pilot a long passionate kiss before he closed the hatch of the hover. I felt a pang of jealousy when she kissed him like that, but I guess it was her way of thanking the guy.

The low humming emerged from the hover, and it slowly rose in the air. I was amazed because I didn't feel any air flow coming from the hover at all. It just hovered in the air!

It started to move away from us, and after we had waved him goodbye she said, "Now we can have some fun!"

CHAPTER SIX.

Like a little girl who had just got her birthday present, she hopped happily to the square package and moved her hand under the sheet of fabric. With a funny smile, she pulled a white ring, which was attached to a string, out of the package.

She cooed, "Now watch this!"

She pulled, with an extremely sexy and elegant tug, on the cord and a loud hissing sound emerged from the now rapidly unfolding package. Within a minute, a dome-shaped tent with a diameter of twelve feet and the height of about seven feet was ready to be used.

I must have opened and shut my mouth at least twice when I saw how fast this enormous dome-shaped tent unfolded itself.

Ellonary clapped her hands with joy and said, "It's always such fun to watch this! Come, have a look inside, you'll be very pleased."

She opened the tent by running her hand along a seam that curled open as if the fabric had shrunk where she had touched it.

I tentatively stepped into the spacious tent that had a soft light at the top that lit the cosy looking interior of the tent. Inside were several warm coloured curtains draped in such a way as to conceal the dome completely. It made the space inside friendly and very inviting.

There was a king-size bed that took up more than half of the space. I crawled on the mattress that was remarkably comfortable and was instantly pushed on my back by Ellonary.

Like a tigress, she crawled over to me with a hungry smile and said, "You know Xander, you have amazed me today."

I couldn't think of what I had done what was so special, and I asked, "Oh? What did I do to amaze you?"

She had a cunning smile when she said huskily, "Take off your clothes and I'll show you what amazes me."

Wow! She knew exactly what she wanted, and I was taken aback by her directness. I felt uneasy because I wasn't used to women pouncing on me in this way, and all I could manage was a nervous stammer, "Wha, what?"

Her hands moved to the top of my shirt, and she opened the zip very slowly while she purred, "You are such a smart boy. Nobody has thought of using a power suit to develop their muscles. And look at this! What a gorgeous pair of pecs you have. I want to feel your biceps and oh, I want to kiss your perfectly shaped abs."

I had noticed other women were looking at me with blatant interest that bordered on desire, and I murmured, "I had worked on that."

She purred and groaned at the same time as she glimpsed sight of my upper body, which was just begging to be admired. Ellonary traced my chest with soft kisses and bit my nipples softly with her teeth. I gasped and moaned with pleasure. I had never felt so aroused.

Her voice was laced with husky breaths, "Your wonderful smell makes me crazy. You are so amazingly hot."

The urge to kiss her was overwhelming, and I wanted to feel her body against mine. I gently took her face between my hands and brought her lips to mine. Those full lips were screaming to be kissed by me.

Only by me.

The first touch of our lips brought sparks into my mind, and I wanted to possess those soft voluptuous lips now and forever. I growled from deep inside me when our passion grew, and I was frustrated by the fact that her top wouldn't open as fast as I wanted it to.

I practically ripped her bra to pieces just so that I could access those wonderful breasts that I only had seen from so far away.

As I slowly teased her hard nipples, she moaned softly, which only made me want her even more. Within moments, I had slipped out of the rest of my clothing and Ellonary helped pull the rest of her suit off of her gorgeous body.

I moved my hands up along her legs while I placed soft kisses on her unbelievable smooth skin. I kissed her belly button and squeezed her warm breasts softly. I finally reached her lips again which I kissed softly while stroking her back.

Her tongue invaded my mouth, and a fiery duel between our tongues made me want her even more. We stopped to get some air, and she said with a tender smile, "That was very nice. Let me get something fun before we continue."

I reluctantly let her go wondering what she had in mind. She crawled away from me to get to her bag. I had a wonderful view of her rear that gleamed softly in the light; I couldn't resist tracing my hand over her well-formed bottom and her toned legs. She giggled and shook her bottom a little before she turned around holding a large ring in her hand.

She slid the ring down at the base of my upright member in one swift move, and it started to shrink until it fitted snug.

It wasn't as cold as I had expected, and it looked kind

of sexy as well. I wondered if it was meant to enhance the sensations, and I asked, "What's that for?"

She twisted the ring clockwise, and it beeped once. As she stroked her hand over her stomach, she said, "I want to keep this flat for a while longer. The ring is to ensure that I don't get pregnant."

I noticed that the ring vibrated a little which enhanced my aroused state even further, and I thought it was a wonderful tool. Trembling with anticipation, my mood was one of euphoria as she began planting small kisses on my stomach before moving onto my chest.

She purred, "I love your strong muscles."

I felt her hard nipples caressing my stomach when she licked my collarbone before gently sinking her teeth into my flesh.

My hands roamed freely over her full breasts. She groaned like a tigress in heat and vigorously attacked my mouth with hers by sucking hard on my bottom lip.

I growled from anticipation when she moved closer, shivering from desire. As she straddled me, she tucked her hair loose which settled like golden waves around her shoulders. She positioned her hips ready for me to enter her and looked into my eyes before saying with a low voice, "You have amazed me for a second time. I like men who can pleasantly surprise me. Do you think you can amaze me more?"

I had amazed myself the last few days, and I was pretty sure that my new nerve system had more surprises I hadn't yet discovered. I stroked her back very lightly with my hands and moved down to her firm yet soft bottom. I squeezed them a little while I said, "Maybe. Let's find out."

She laughed softly and bit the top of my nose, "We'll start slow. Don't come before the ring has beeped twice."

I nodded eagerly, feeling the radiating heat of her nether parts on my member. So close!

She moaned softly when she moved down on me slowly welcoming my rock hard tool into her silky wet smooth hotness. I felt her tunnel eagerly engulf my member, and she gasped when I was fully in her, "It feels so wonderful. I've been dreaming about this nearly every night since I've seen your manhood bulging so majestically from the power suit."

I moved my hands to her breasts and unexpectedly pinched her nipples. She yelped, and I said, "That was the most exciting and horrible moment I ever had experienced."

She giggled and tensed the muscles in her vagina causing me to rumble with pleasure. She whispered in my ear, "Punish me if you dare."

That little sentence drove me wild, and I had to move, I needed to feel her inner parts squeeze my cock again. I heard the ring beep twice, and I started to move my body in a steady rhythm. She kissed me tenderly and said mischievously, "Oh, you want to be in control even when I'm on top."

I smiled, "This is just a warm up."

She sounded like an animal when she purred, "Oh my! Bring it on, my super-hot Anix."

I growled and increased the speed that I was moving in and out.

I was sure I could punish her by making her beg for more.

****

I was awakened by a soft beeping sound. I felt that my Little Alex wasn't that little anymore, and I felt a warm and soft body next to me.

Then it dawned on me where I was. I was in the tent with the beautiful hot nurse Ellonary.

I assumed that the beep came from the ring around my shaft. I touched the ring that was smooth to the touch, and I noticed a certain soreness in the delicate parts of my member.

She was still sleeping which didn't surprise me after the night we'd enjoyed. My enhanced nerve system proved to be fantastic for both parties. I could control the timing of my orgasms, and the speed I could pound into her was incredible. I was glad that we were out in the open, far away from civilisation. They would have been thumping at my door if we were having the same kind of fun in my room. I had lost count of how many times she had climaxed, but I was sure that I had "amazed" Ellonary enough.

A soft hand moved over my chest, and when it arrived at my neck, it pulled me towards a pair of soft lips. She kissed me tenderly on my lips and said with a croaky voice, "Good morning."

I kissed her back and said, "Morning Ellonary."

She stretched her body against mine while she sighed with contentment, moaning softly.

I caressed her back and asked, "You're okay?"

"I feel amazing, but I'm also really sore."

"Oh dear, I'm sorry."

She hugged me hard and nibbled at one of my nipples. She giggled, "Nobody has done me that hard and for such a long time! I lost count how many times I had climaxed, but I have loved every second of it."

A smiled appeared on my lips, and I asked, "So, did I amaze you enough?"

She snuggled up to me even closer and said huskily, "Oh yes. Yes, definitely."

The ring beeped twice, and she mumbled in my neck, "Hmmm, tempting, but I think I'll pass this time."

I kissed her hair feeling extremely content at having her so close to me, and I said, "Hmmm, I think you're right."

She sighed when I stroked her back with my free hand as I remembered what we had done last night.

The next thing I knew she got up with a jolt and exclaimed, "We need to get dressed, I hear hovers coming, and they will be here in a few moments!"

A pulsating low humming was clearly audible, and Ellonary grabbed her suit. Without any underwear, she wrestled herself into the suit and within a few seconds she had it zipped closed. After a few ferocious strokes with her fingers through her hair, she looked like a sensual goddess, and she climbed out the tent as the hovers were descending.

I was amazed at how quickly she was able to get dressed. Then I realised that she was a nurse, and she probably had to be able to get ready in an emergency.

Meanwhile, I managed to get myself into the power suit that was fifty-percent charged. It took me about a minute to make myself presentable enough to crawl out of the tent as well.

Next to the hovers were a few people waiting who I didn't recognise but I was pleased to see Ellonary talking to the healing master and that Estrella wasn't there. I felt guilty that I had spent this incredible night with Ellonary.

When I joined them, the healing master looked at me with a broad smile. "I heard you managed to drain the battery from the power suit. I never thought it was possible."

"Yes, I think I was a little bit too enthusiastic yesterday."

The healing master chuckled and said, "I think you need to change the settings. There must be an option to charge the power suit when you're using it for strengthening your muscles. Have a look in the menu tab "power saving". That might fix your issue."

I found the option in the menu and switched it on. I moved my arm, and I noticed the slight resistance increase and I remembered that I had seen another setting that regulates the charging capacity. From now on the power suit would always be charged so long as I was moving my body.

Ellonary asked the healing master, "I assume research had fun with the Anix?"

"Yes, they were only puzzled by the pieces of fabric on its tongue."

I laughed and said while pointing at my frayed trousers, "Well, the Anix was hoping to have me as its dinner."

The healing master said, "Oh my, you had to face an Anix as well? Dear Xander, you've been very lucky."

The healing master's surprise amused me, and I said with a gleam, "If Ellonary weren't such a good shooter I wouldn't have been able to tell you what had happened."

Ellonary blushed a little and said, "I was just there at the right time."

The healing master said, "Just as well. Just as well Ellonary. Hmmm, Now Xander, can I have a short talk with you? Face to face."

I was curious as to what he wanted to talk about, and I said to him while we walked away from the rest, "Of course healing master, what is on your mind?"

He looked at me with a serious expression and said, "There are two things that are bothering me, Xander. The first is the enormous amount of energy your body can generate. I know you take enough calories in food with you, but your strength is still roughly four hundred percent what it should be."

Four hundred percent! My body is using an insane amount of energy, and so I asked him, "Do you think something is not right?"

"I don't know Xander. Maybe you should stop training your body so vigorously for a few days and see what happens."

The fact that I had managed to drain a power suit made me take his suggestion seriously, and I said, "I guess that might be interesting. I hope that I don't suffer from withdraw symptoms too much."

He laughed and said, "You can still do some light exercises if you can't sit still."

"I can deal with that for a few days."

"Good." He said while placing a hand on my shoulder,

and I saw his face turn even more serious. He thought long and hard for a moment and then he said, "I'm afraid I have to address a delicate issue that I rather wouldn't but since I'm her spirit guide I have no option."

Oh, shit! He wanted to talk about Estrella! Instantly my pleasant and relaxed state changed into the well-known knot in my stomach. Out of respect for him I didn't want to end the conversation straight away, and I said in a respectful tone, "I assume you're referring to Estrella and me."

The expression on my face clearly made him choose his words carefully. "Well, Yes. You see, Estrella is young and quite impulsive and doesn't always understand the consequences of her actions. Most of the time I have been able to advise her, and everything works out okay. However, this time her judgement has been clouded by something that she has never previously experienced."

I started to get the picture, and I suddenly felt horrible. I had been a real asshole. I asked softly, "Does this involve me?"

He smiled somewhat sadly and said, "I'm afraid so."

I was shocked. "Oh, shit."

The healing master raised his eyebrows and said, "I don't see the relation with faeces but yes, she has it bad. A promise has to be fulfilled, no matter who she is."

"Well, I think I made a promise to her mother as well."

"Did you really?"

"Well uh, yes I did."

He shook his head. "Estrella didn't mention that at all. She has it bad my boy. She has it bad. Please be gentle with her. I don't want to spend the last periods of my service trying to heal a broken heart."

I didn't know what to make of it, and I asked, "Tell me, what did Estrella promise her mother exactly?"

His answer was short, "That you would attempt the regeneration ceremony."

Again! What was it about this bloody regeneration

ceremony! Everyone placed so much emphasis on this! I was getting increasingly frustrated, and I said, "Why is this ceremony so special?"

He attempted to hide his emotions, "None of the contestants has ever survived the ceremony."

This was worse than I had feared! I blew out some air. What was going on at this strange planet? I had no idea, and I asked, "Why not?"

"The ones who opted to take the test failed."

"Why would you choose to do the test?"

He looked at me as if he didn't believe that I had asked that question, and he said gruffly, "If you want to become a legal Yourien and stay here of course!"

Now the hoo-ha of it all sunk in. Estrella wanted me to stay, and therefore I had to do this test!

I stopped walking, and muttered, "This is insane!"

"The situation that you find yourself in is indeed grave."

"I want to know exactly what I get myself into if I'm going to do this test."

His face turned pale, and he said with a tremor in his voice, "That is the problem. We don't know."

I laughed in disbelief, and I asked, "Okay, who *does* know?"

"Nobody, except The Highest."

I more or less had expected that answer, and I sighed. "Great. I have to do a test that nobody else has ever survived, just to be able to stay?"

"Yes."

Even though I already knew the answer, I still needed to be sure. "What if I don't want to do the test?"

He said quite sternly, "You will have to leave our planet at the earliest possible opportunity."

Which I knew was in twenty days.

I asked him, "Do you think I would have a chance of surviving the test?"

He looked down when he said, "Considering how the

other contestants have died I think you might have a small chance."

I knew he wasn't allowed to answer my next question, but I asked it anyway. "How did they die?"

He nearly whispered, "I'm sorry Xander, but I'm not allowed to reveal that information. The only thing I can say is that you have a major advantage, and there is a possibility that you might survive the test."

So there was hope for me *if* I decided to do this necessary test. I sighed and retorted, "I need to think about it."

His voice was dark when he said, "You have until the new lunar in seven cycles."

"What will happen if I decide I want to do the test?"

Clearly he had some difficulty speaking the words without getting emotional. "If you decide to do the test you need a sponsor. Once a sponsor has been assigned you can do the test."

I instantly knew that Estrella was my sponsor, and I asked, "Can I choose my sponsor?"

He cleared his throat and said softly, "It has been already decided that Estrella is to be your sponsor, and I'm afraid you can't change that anymore. You should have done that at the last new lunar. But, you should also know that Estrella only just made it in the nick of time to submit her request."

I didn't expect that answer at all!

Now I understood what had happened.

She had no choice!

She wanted me to stay, and this was the only way that it would ever be possible. I now truly regretted behaving like an asshole and snapping at her.

I turned to look at the old man, and I smiled, "Thank you, for telling me. You have cleared a lot of stuff up for me. I think I want to go back to the city on foot. It will give me some more time to think about it."

He grabbed both of my hands and said in a pleading

voice, "You are a sensible man. Please speak with Estrella as soon as possible."

I knew it was going to be difficult, but it would help me to make the right decision. I conceded, "Yes healing master, I will talk to Estrella."

His face cleared up as if a huge weight had been lifted from his shoulders, and he said coarsely, "Good. Now, considering how nurse Ellonary came out of the dome I assume that you weren't just sleeping."

My face turned bright red and before I could say anything else he continued, "You should know that monogamy is seldom practiced in our society and that we are very open when it comes to sexual relationships. Did you use the ring?"

I stammered, "Yes, yes we did."

He smiled, "Good. If you decide to stay you must tell Estrella you have a relationship with Ellonary as well before taking the test."

He continued because he saw my troubled expression, "Don't worry, Estrella and Ellonary are very good friends."

This wasn't the first time that I had felt very uncomfortable but I had no idea what I was supposed to think about the healing master's revelation about the lack of monogamy on this planet. It opened a whole new dimension of possibilities!

But then I thought about it for a minute, and I dismissed it.

It would never happen.

It was too good to be true; having Estrella *and* Ellonary as lovers.

We were back at the hovers and I saw that Ellonary was already sitting in one of them looking beautiful after our long wonderful night. I climbed in beside her and found myself gazing adoringly at her lovely face.

Her face lit up, and she snuggled up to me while asking with a pleading expression on her face, "Are you going to sit next to me?"

I was torn in two. I wanted to stay with her, but I also needed the time to set my mangled thoughts straight. I took her hand and said, "No, sorry. Not this time. I'm going to run back to the city. I need time to think about a few things."

She kissed my lips and whispered, "I would love to wash your body when you arrive."

I chuckled and squeezed her hand a little when I said, "I bet you would. See you later Ellonary."

I gave her a long and passionate kiss before I jumped out the hover, and I started my journey back to the city.

I felt re-energized by our hot kiss.

CHAPTER SEVEN.

During my run back to the city, I came to the conclusion that I could do the test. The healing master was keeping something from me, and I guessed that it had to do with my treatment with the Garntuoa nerve.

There was one major question that had to be answered before I could make the right decision; why was I on this planet?

Without that vital piece of information, I might easily choose to return home. I knew for sure that Estrella had the answer to that question, and I doubted if she would give me an answer I could accept.

****

Freshly washed and shaven I headed to the healing master's office, hoping that he could arrange a meeting with Estrella.

Just as I was about to enter the office, I bumped into Estrella. It was all that I could do to prevent our heads from colliding but our bodies touched, and I managed to prevent her falling against the wall by grabbing her arm.

She staggered backwards, and when she saw it was me,

her face turned bright red. She stammered, "I, I'm sorry. I should have looked where I was walking."

I seized the moment, "That's okay. I wanted to talk to you."

She gasped, and she said in a hoarse voice, "I'm not sure if."

I felt as though I was on the cusp of losing this special moment, and I interrupted her while I tried to get her at ease, "Look, Estrella, I want to apologise. I've been a jerk."

She regained some of her self-esteem and said softly, "I don't know what you mean."

I saw a glimpse of her affection for me in her eyes, and I knew I had to apologise for what I had done wrong. I said softly, "I never gave you the opportunity to explain, and I'm sorry that I compared you with your mother."

Her beautiful smile appeared on her face and she tried to grumble, "Comparing me with my mother was unforgivable."

Feeling joyful, I said apologetically, "You have half of her genes."

She pouted her lips, and I quickly said, "And you've got the best half."

"Don't use up all your charms. You might need them later."

Yes!

I was forgiven!

Now I had to strike while the iron was hot! I laughed, and I said, "I wouldn't dare to hurt my sponsor again."

Her face instantly changed into a concerned look, "Are you sure you want to do the test?"

During our conversation I had directed us to the gardens of the complex and I knew pretty sure we could talk freely. I looked her straight in her eyes, and I asked, "Estrella, why did I end up here?"

She quickly looked down and said, "I can't tell you that."

Shit! I had to have the answer, and I said, "I remember

you asking the healing master to give me something to make me better."

She gasped but said nothing.

I knew that I needed to be a little more diplomatic. Sighing, I said, "Look, Estrella, I understand that you can't reveal everything but did you bring me here?"

Her eyes were wet when she nodded, "I couldn't let you die."

I started to understand what might have happened. Estrella believed that she was responsible for the fact that I had been struck by lightning.

She felt guilty!

I sincerely hoped she wasn't, "Are you feeling guilty about what happened to me?"

"At first I did, but then you were so cheerful and when I made that mistake." She closed her eyes in embarrassment and shook her head a little.

She looked up and took my hand as she said, "You showed me that things could be different."

I was relieved by her answer but also a bit taken aback. I still wasn't satisfied with the situation, and I needed more clarity. I cleared my throat, and I had to ask her directly, "Estrella, do *you* want me to stay here?"

My heart was pounding when she hesitated for a moment. She stared at the ground, and then she started to talk really slow as if she wanted to make no mistakes in what she was going to say, "My selfish part says: 'yes' but my heart says: I don't want you to risk your life for me."

Shocked by her unexpectedly honest answer I said, "You have a point there, and I will be honest with you too. I don't know if I'm eager enough to stay. But we have seven cycles to find out."

She whimpered softly as if she was in pain and croaked, "We only have three cycles where we can be together, Xander. The last four are taken by your preparation of the test that you will be alone to overthink your decision."

I was shocked again: four bloody days alone? I started

to doubt if I wanted to be a part of this stupid world.

She saw my disbelief and said, "It means that I, as the sponsor, am not allowed to be with you so that your mind is not influenced by me."

I had to admit that it made sense, and I said with some remorse, "I see."

She grabbed my hand and said cheerfully, "Come, we mustn't waste what little time we have remaining by complaining. There's much to do. Let me show you how to fight with the stick."

Her switch to a cheerful person made me wonder how it would be if we would be together for a longer time. A smile lit up my face, and I said, "I never have guessed you're into martial art."

She raised her eyebrows and said with an authoritative voice like her mother, "Dear Alex, you don't even know the smallest thing about me. Prepare to be awed."

I laughed and while I bowed I said, "My Lady, please show me your wonders."

****

I had lost count of how many times Estrella managed to get me down onto the practice mat, but she made clear I was far from ready to face the challenge. I was too amazed by her fabulous body to see even the first few blows coming.

Estrella usually dressed in loose fitting tops and long skirts that as the daughter of The Highest she was required to wear.

When she entered the practice hall, I had to look twice before I realised it was her. She was dressed in an ultra-thin snug fitting training suit and she had the cutest behind I had ever seen; nicely round and firm. I saw that she was wearing a sports bra that flattened her breasts, but I could see that they were a little smaller than Ellonary's. She moved her beautiful toned body so gracefully that I wanted to gaze at it for hours.

She had to laugh at the first two times when she painfully brought me down to the matt. She knew I was distracted by her revealing outfit but after the third time she planted her foot on my chest and asked, "Do you want to see me only for the next three cycles or do you want to enjoy my company a lot longer?"

That question brought me back to the purpose of this session, and I tried to focus on the technique she was demonstrating. The weapon was an unbreakable stick of about four feet long and a half inch in diameter. It felt like a rod of wood, and the ends hadn't been sharpened but if you were fast enough you could punch through someone's neck with it. The rods we used for our practice sessions had padded ends that I was extremely grateful for.

After our session, Estrella gave me a demonstration of her skills. She gracefully fought against a robot, and she used the stick as if it was an extension of her body. Within one minute, the robot had lost its arms and was punctured through the neck. I would never have thought that a simple stick could be such a fatal weapon.

Her smile was mesmerising when she saw that I was completely stunned by her performance. She walked to me and asked while she was panting a little, "You want to try it as well?"

I knew I could do some tricks but what she had done was way beyond my capabilities even with my enhanced nerve system.

I answered softly, "I think I will pass for the moment."

She saw my doubt and said encouragingly, "Please try it, Xander. I know you can do more than you give yourself credit for. I've seen your incredibly fast reactions."

I knew that I had to go for it: any experience I could get might be my saviour at the regeneration ceremony, and I said, "Okay, but can you set the fighting level of the robot a bit lower?"

She laughed, and as she patted my back, she said, "Of

course. We don't want you to be crippled before the test, do we?"

I grinned and grunted sarcastically, "Funny Estrella, very funny."

She giggled as she summoned the assistant for a new robot.

The robot was floating like a hover, and its arms were as thin as a stick with human-like hands at the end. The head of the robot was expressionless, and the eyes were clearly two cameras.

Estrella prepared the robot, and when she was finished, she said, "I think you can beat it with some effort."

The robot floated towards me and moved its stick ready to hit my arm. I easily managed to dodge the attack, by kicking it away with my foot.

Estrella exclaimed happily, "Nice combination!"

The robot came back, and before it could attack me, I swung my stick to hit its neck. Just before the stick hit the robot, it swung incredibly fast and moved towards me with such a speed that I was barely able to avoid being hit.

I couldn't believe what had just happened, but I didn't have time to think about it because the robot was swinging its stick extremely fast while it barged straight at me. I felt the air flow of the stick passing my eye as I managed to hit the stick away.

This robot was too fast for me, and all I could do was avoid the hit.

I could see that Estrella was getting involved in the fight as well, and she managed to sever the arm with the stick of the robot. As nothing was happening the robot flew directly at me, and I dodged the attack by kicking the robot full in its body. I was proud of the fact that I had at least managed to make a large dent in it, as I saw Estrella puncture its neck.

Something was clearly wrong because the robot continued to attack me. However, the puncture to its neck must have damaged some of its functionality, and I had just enough time to swing my stick. With an enormous roar, I smacked the rod against its head. The head flew off the torso of the robot and smashed against the wall in pieces.

Estrella rushed to me and said, "You are hurt. We need to go to the healing master!"

I was surprised because I thought the robot hadn't hit me, and I felt nothing but then I realised that drops of blood were dripping from my right eye. Aware that Estrella was distressed, I said reassuringly, "It's nothing, just a small cut. But what happened with that robot?"

She said wearily, "I don't know, something must have malfunctioned."

We both jumped when the robot suddenly started to hiss, and purple flames sprouted out of its neck.

I knew now for sure that someone had tampered with the robot and wanted to be sure that there was no evidence to be found.

Estrella pulled me away from the robot and said, "You need to go to the healing master. Once we know that you are unharmed, we can begin to figure out who is trying to kill you."

Her comment made me suddenly aware that something definitely wasn't right. I could hardly believe that someone wanted me harmed, but everything so far was inevitably gearing towards that direction.

Damn! What the hell was going on?

When we arrived at the healing master, the whole complex was in a state of alarm. The fire of the robot had triggered a whole range of different alarms. It seemed that it had been a long time since there was a fire in the complex, and it was clear that the authorities didn't really know how to deal with it.

While the healing master was cleaning my cut, he asked, "What happened? Did you two have a fight?"

Estrella huffed, "Do you think I would harm him?"

I chuckled and said, "No, a training robot was

compromised, and it tried to kill me."

While he sealed the wound with a little tube, he said, "That is a rather serious accusation. Are you sure?"

Estrella said gruffly, "It still attacked Xander after I had managed to puncture its neck."

He raised his eyebrows as he was clearing his gear away and said, "Hmmm, that sounds like that somebody managed to overrule the robot's program. I really would like to investigate it."

I said, "I don't think you will find much because it went up in flames."

His eyes grew bigger, and he said, "Somebody with access to secure areas wants you dead. We need to be very cautious."

I started to ponder. Who wanted me dead and why? I had the feeling that I had been in this situation before, and I didn't like it at all.

I felt Estrella's hand on my shoulder, and she said, "We need to find you another place to sleep."

"Yes, but where?" I replied.

Ellonary's husky voice filled the room, "He is always welcome to sleep with me."

We all turned to her. She was standing dressed in her usual nurse suit leaning against the wall looking at me with greedy eyes.

I gulped because I thought her voice sounded a bit too eager and I was speechless when I heard Estrella reply, "That's fine but only if you let him sleep."

I couldn't believe what Estrella just had said, and the girls started to laugh when they saw my astonished expression.

The healing master shrugged his shoulders when I glanced at him and said, "I haven't said anything."

I looked at Ellonary and then at Estrella and I asked Estrella, "You knew about Ellonary and me?"

Estrella giggled when Ellonary started to blush profoundly while she stuttered, "I was uh supposed to have a training session with Estrella this morning. I had to confess to her that you and I had spent the night together because I was in no shape to do the training."

Now it was my turn to blush when Estrella said, "I was waiting for you to tell me, but I guess you never had the chance."

I didn't know what to say, and I felt so stupid! Apparently Estrella didn't mind I had spent the night with Ellonary, which was still hard to believe.

I sighed. "Estrella, I'm sorry I didn't tell you."

She smiled, and light-heartedly said, "Apology accepted Xander. Now, we need to hurry because my mother expects us to be there on time for the introduction."

Oh no. No more surprises! My mind was boggled and I asked with a sigh, "Introduction?"

I could see Estrella panicking a bit when she said, "Err yes, I forgot to tell you. As your sponsor, I have to introduce you officially to the court."

Ellonary said reassuringly, "Go, Estrella, I'll take care of him."

Estrella clearly relieved hugged her and said, "Thanks, I'll send his costume to your place."

As she walked away, she turned around once more and said, "Behave you two! It's important that you are on time Xander!"

Ellonary sighed and said, "Where is her trust? I can keep my hands off you if I have to."

I laughed so hard that tears started falling from my eyes.

CHAPTER EIGHT.

We stopped by my room to get some personal items and I had a short shower because I had little time left to get dressed. Ellonary insisted on washing my back but kept her promise to Estrella and made sure that I didn't get too aroused. I had to smile. In washing my back she got what she wanted. I vowed one day to ask her why she wanted to wash my back.

Luckily my outfit turned out to be a normal three-piece suit, and it fitted perfectly. I would have been dressed in no time if Ellonary hadn't kept fiddling with my hair with the result that I ended up rushing.

Estrella was waiting for me, and I was very surprised when I saw her. She looked drop dead gorgeous in her snug fitting gala dress that was clearly designed to show her slim figure. Her makeup was delicate accentuating her beautiful eyes. She smiled when she saw me and marvelled, "I never thought you could look so amazing in a traditional costume."

I chuckled. "Well, you look stunning as well. We are going to be *the* pair of the evening."

She murmured softly, "Yes, I think my mother will be pleased. It is the custom that the sponsor is engaging during the conversations. You might have to answer a question or two."

I squeezed her hand and said, "Let's hope it stays at just a few questions."

As we walked into the hall, I saw her mother standing on a raised platform. A voice shouted, "The Fille of The Highest."

I was amazed that Estrella was announced, and I felt all the eyes of the people in the hall drop on us. Everybody was silent and bowed for Estrella as we solemnly strode to her mother. I could see that most of the women were looking at me with great interest. Some of them I recognised but a few I didn't and they were clearly impressed by what they saw passing by. It hammered home the fact that like it or not, people do judge someone on their appearance, and I was forced to admit to myself that I was guilty of doing the same.

I wondered if her mother was wearing the same makeup that she had been wearing when we first met, and as we drew closer to her, I realised that she looked as hideous as ever.

As we stood still in front of the platform Estrella bowed for her mother, and I followed her in a split second.

Her mother said with a forceful voice, "My Fille."

Estrella replied somewhat annoyed, "Your Highest."

Estrella's mother looked me up and down and said, "I see you brought your sponsored guest. I must admit he looks a lot more promising."

Estrella gasped in anger and cleared her throat before she said sarcastically, "Thank you for your compliment Your Highest."

I admired Estrella's fierce look whereby her eyes were squinted to a small line. I assumed her mother would sneer back at her, but she addressed me instead by asking, "I've heard you managed to survive an encounter with an Anix."

I should have known! She was using me to defuse the

precarious moment she had created. I looked up at her, and I said, "Yes, Your Highest. I was lucky."

She raised her eyebrows. "I guess you were. Now, my daughter still thinks you're willing to do the test."

Ah, what a bitch! I thought it was a nasty way to change the conversation, and I didn't want to dignify it with a response. I was very relieved when I heard Estrella say placidly, "We are still in a discussion about it Your Highest."

All the people in the hall were looking at Estrella's mother who started to chuckle softly. She said, "My Fille, always keeping all her options open until the last moment."

Again! I thought she was a real bitch to use her daughter's official title again. She was a master at stirring delicate matters, and I knew I was taking a risk but I had to say it, "With all due respect, Your Highest, this time it was *me* who wanted more time to consider."

I heard several people gasp, and Estrella was so shocked that she let go of my hand. I didn't care, and I was willing to take full responsibility for my actions. In my opinion, Estrella's mother needed to tone herself down a bit even if she was The Highest. I hated those stupid power games.

The hall was silent, and the tension was building by the second until her mother said with a small smile, "It suits you, to be bold. I appreciate your defence for my daughter."

Relieved I let go of the breath that I had been holding. I hid my smile when I bowed. "Thank you, Your Highest."

She clapped her hands and said, "Very well. Let the food be served."

Estrella grinned from ear to ear when I dared to look at her. She moved close to me and whispered in my ear, "You've written history. Nobody would even dream of doing what you've just done. Thank you."

I felt the heavy chunks of anxiety falling off my

shoulder, and I breathed, "You're welcome; I didn't think it was fair the way in which she was speaking to you."

Her mother descended from the raised platform and strode to a long table at the other end of the hall. I let Estrella lead me to my place, and I was surprised that I was seated opposite her mother.

I saw that many of the men had put their jacket at the back of their chair, and I was more than happy to do the same. I thought it was really hot in the hall.

There was clearly some excitement at the table when I removed my jacket and they saw my sculptured torso which up until this point had been hidden by the jacket.

As I draped my jacket on the chair I noticed that little crinkles of smoke were coming out of the collar of my jacket. I knew now that I wasn't imagining the fact that the belt of my trousers was getting hot as well.

Something in the fabric was getting very hot.

I needed water to cool the jacket and my trousers down!

Frantically looking around, I saw a small fountain situated in the corner of the hall. I grabbed the jacket from the chair that was now smoking heavily, and I ran as fast as I could to the water.

I jumped into the fountain with an enormous splash hoping that the water would stop my belt from getting hotter, and somehow, I managed to extinguish the now burning jacket.

It all happened in such a short space of time that I was simply relieved to be able to run so fast. I was shocked by how hot the jacket had become in such a short time.

The only thing I hated right now was that I had the attention of all the people in the hall. Here I was, sitting in my fancy clothes in the pompous fountain with a jet of water pouring over my head.

I could see Estrella's mother trying her best not to laugh out loud as she summoned the security to help me out my awkward situation.

Armed with big towels three men helped me out of the fountain and hurried me to a small room at the back of the hall.

One of the men addressed me in an authoritative way, "Take off those pants immediately. The water only delays the chemical reaction."

I practically ripped the pants of me because I indeed noticed that the belt was getting hotter by every second. Just as I had them off, the bright purple flames ate the fabric of the pants away.

I couldn't believe my eyes! The colour of the flames was exactly the same as the colour of the flames that came out the fighting robot. I was now certain that this was the work of the same person who had tried killing me earlier.

The head of security said, "This chemical has been banned for so long that most of our staff doesn't know of its existence. The person who is trying to harm you is either old or has a keen interest in dangerous weapons."

I mused, "I think it's the latter. It must be someone with a profound knowledge of tactical weaponry and substantial knowledge as to how to bypass your security."

"Hmm, there are a few people who might fit that profile but it still doesn't make sense. What would be the motive?"

I had been thinking about it, but I hadn't found a valid reason as to why a person would want me to fail unless they didn't want me to be together with Estrella or Ellonary. Something I found hard to believe in a society that didn't believe in monogamy.

An assistant came into the room with a new set of clothes and the man carefully sniffed at the collar of the jacket. He said as he handed the jacket, "Smell the jacket. Do you notice the difference?"

I inhaled the smell of the fabric, and there was a difference, but I couldn't discern what. I said, "Yes, but what is different I can't tell."

He smiled and said, "That is the danger of this

chemical that has a very suitable nickname "Sweet-Pepper". It has a subtle hint of sweet candy that has a comforting effect."

I pondered about the name; it juiced up my evening! Meanwhile, I was nearly dressed again, and I said, "I assume we will have another talk after this show?"

His white teeth looked fake when he smiled, and he said, "Yes if The Highest allows me to talk to you. Now hurry, she doesn't like to look at an empty chair for so long."

I wasn't surprised, and I murmured to myself as I walked into the hall again, "I'll bloody well show her I don't like this stupid event at all."

I walked down to my chair acting as if nothing had happened. When I sat down Estrella's mother looked at me with a funny smile and moved forward to me to ask, "I assume you had a talk with my head of security?"

I nodded, "Yes, Your Highest. I really would like to have another talk with him. Someone clearly doesn't want me here."

Her remark was utterly shocking, "Yes, and he is not the only one."

I couldn't believe what she just had said! I wanted to know more, but she moved back from me and got up while she raised her glass.

Everyone got up from their seats and raised their glass as well.

She spoke with a powerful voice while looking at me with a twinkle in her eye, "As Your Highest I wish you all a good health and prosperity. I also wish the introduced faith, strength and endurance for his challenge and we wish him good luck."

All the guests were looking at me and when Estrella started to applaud the whole Hall joined her and I felt extremely uncomfortable to be in the centre of it all.

I was still totally shocked by what Estrella's mother had said to me, "He is not the only one."

Did she know who was trying to kill me?

Who else didn't want me to stay?

What the hell was going on?

I saw her looking at me with a cunning grin because she saw that I was shocked by her bold statement. She bowed slightly towards me and said without being discrete, "Being fast is not enough to keep yourself alive."

When she saw my reaction, she laughed and strode away leaving her guests alone.

I truly hated it when people dropped a bombshell and then just left you with the shattered pieces.

What the hell was this about?

Why was she revealing this information to me?

She clearly knew much more than I thought she would. But why didn't she act upon the danger I was facing?

I still didn't get it: Why was I a target?

What had I done wrong?

Estrella took my hand and whispered in my ear, "I want to leave as soon as possible. Eat something off your plate and then we are allowed to leave."

The burdened words of her mother kept ringing in my ears: "He is not the only one", "Being fast won't keep you alive."

I was starting to get paranoid, and I was convinced that my food had been poisoned as well. I didn't want to take the risk, and I needed a distraction. I acted clumsily and I knocked my glass of wine over the untouched food on my plate. I had to jump off my chair to stop the wine from staining my trousers.

Estrella had trouble not giggling and reached for my hand when she said, "Let's go. You've had enough."

I was more than pleased to leave the judgemental crowd behind, and I admitted. "Yes, I surely have."

As we rushed out the hall, I followed Estrella because I hadn't a clue where she was heading until we ended up in the largest kitchen I have ever seen.

One of the ladies walked to Estrella with a warm smile

on her face. She hugged her and said, "Hello my pumpkin, who is this extremely handsome guy?"

Estrella blushed a little when she said, "I'm his sponsor."

The lady looked me straight in the eyes and asked, "Have you eaten already?"

I looked at Estrella, who said, "We could eat some more."

A grin appeared on the lady's face as she guided us to the huge table in the middle of the kitchen while she shouted, "Two special dinners please!"

****

I had never felt so stuffed in all of my life, but I was grateful that I now knew a place where I could eat without any worries.

I still didn't tell Estrella what her mother had said to me because I didn't know what to make of it.

Was her mother just teasing me or was she telling me the truth?

It was hard to make any decisions based on the poor amount of information. It was hard to imagine why anyone would want to eliminate me. Staying with Ellonary was the best option for now.

Estrella brought me to Ellonary's quarters, and we stood opposite each other, not knowing what to say. She sighed and said as if nothing had happened, "It was a very interesting day."

I smiled at her funny understatement, and I conceded, "Yes, it was."

She kissed me quickly on my cheek and said, "Goodnight Xander."

I felt something when she kissed me and I wanted to take her in my arms and kiss her properly, but I respected her conservation. I gave her a warm smile and said, "Goodnight, see you in the morning."

I sneaked into Ellonary's room and I quickly got undressed. I was exhausted by all the events, and I was looking forward to a good sleep. As I slipped into the bed next to Ellonary's warm body she turned around and hugged me from behind while kissing me on my neck. I heard her murmuring, "You took your time."

I played with the idea of having sex, but I was too tired and too preoccupied with all the strange things that had happened.

I kissed her hand and whispered, "Go to sleep. I'll entertain you tomorrow."

She spooned even closer up to my back and placed her hand on my chest as she sighed in contentment. The warmth of her body made me sleepy and before I knew it I was asleep.

CHAPTER NINE.

I woke up with a start because I dreamt I was lying in bed drenched with the chemical Sweet-Pepper. I guess I smelled the sweet perfume of Ellonary on the pillow I was lying on. I was alone lying on the huge bed, and I found a tablet lying on the other pillow.

I picked it up, and it started to play a recorded message from her. Her pretty face looked so sexy as she whispered, "Hi Xander. I knew you would be totally exhausted from our wonderful night and the introduction. I had promised Estrella to let you sleep."

She turned the camera to the bed where I was lying on my stomach with my back exposed. She turned the camera back and said, "I forgot to tell you I had an early shift, and if you look at the top left corner you'll know when I'll be back. I'm afraid that by the time I finish work, you'll already be gone. See you later, my Sweet-Pepper."

She sighed and blew me a kiss.

I dropped the tablet, and I jumped out the bed.

My heart was in my throat.

Had she used Sweet-Pepper as a nickname or was it a hint?

I sniffed the air in her room, and I'm not sure if I

smelled the deceiving sweet smell of the dangerous chemical which made me feel trapped. I desperately wanted to take a shower, but I didn't dare to leave the room in case something would catch fire.

The timid knock at the door was so welcome that I rushed to open it without realising that I only was wearing my briefs.

Estrella was at the door, and when I saw her eyes sizing me up and down, I felt my cheeks turning red hot. She smiled and gave me a long gentle hug. "Good morning Xander. I hope you had a good sleep."

I loved the way she dealt with the awkward situation, and I said, "Yes, not bad. I was just going to take a quick shower."

"Oh okay. Can I wait here for you to get ready?"

I had great trouble hiding my relief when I replied, "Yes, of course, why not. Uhm, I'll be done in a few moments."

I normally like to take a leisurely shower but this time I slipped into the spray of warm water and washed myself as quickly as possible.

When I returned, Estrella was sitting on the bed with the tablet in her hand. She had a grin on her face when she said, "Poor Ellonary."

I laughed, "She is a real nice woman. I can see why you are close friends with her."

Estrella's face turned bright red and she tried to change the subject by saying, "Yes, are you hungry?"

I was intrigued by Estrella's reaction, but my hunger triggered my animal instinct and overruled the urge to ask any further questions. I said simply, "Like an Anix."

****

After my training session with Estrella, I decided to have a few hours running with my power suit on. I needed some time alone. It was strange strapping myself in the suit again after I had been out of it for a while.

As I was checking my straps, I remembered the training I had with Estrella. She'd brought me to a secluded and private training hall that was part of her mother's quarters. I thought that she wanted be alone with me but when she showed me the next level of our training I understood why we used this secluded hall.

Estrella was as fast if not faster than me, and I attributed this to her weight. I was much heavier because of my higher muscle mass. It was amazing how we could move so fast and still be so accurate. It took a lot of energy, but training with an equal was incredibly satisfying even though it left me with a few gnawing questions:

Why was she as fast as me?

Were the Garntuoas connected with the Youriens?

Did they have the same ancestors?

Was Estrella somebody special?

I had asked her about the Garntuoas, but she was unwilling or unable to give me any information about them at all. When we stopped our training session I had more questions than answers which I found very frustrating.

I double checked the power suit, and I had chosen my favourite route that had several long straight stretches of road and a few steep hills. The first part of the route was straight through a dense forest that was in the shade. It was always a little bit cooler there which was perfect to start training.

The first stretch of road was just long enough to warm my muscles and the second stretch didn't kick in until after the two hills. When I arrived at the second stretch of road, I felt my muscles longing for the power sprint I was planning to do. I started to increase my pace, accelerating to a comfortable speed. There was a gentle curve in the road, and when I was halfway along the curve, I saw something lying on the road. The closer I got the more certain I was that it was a body lying straight across the road. The person was wearing a white suit with red accents.

Boy was I wrong!

As I got closer, I saw a female lying face down. Her white suit was stained with her blood. Her long brown hair lay partially in a dark pool of her blood. Her wrist had dark red welts, and her neck was covered with dark marks. This woman had been murdered!

My mind was racing, as I asked myself just why she had been dumped on a road and not in the forest.

Why on this road? Was it because I had been using this more often?

I looked in the menu of my power suit and turned on the emergency locator. I deliberately kept as far away from the body as possible in order not to disturb any evidence. However, I knew for certain that she was dumped from a hover.

Within ten minutes, the humming noise of the hovers was clearly audible. It didn't take them long to arrive!

The two hovers landed just a few feet away from me, and the head of security was the first to get out.

He asked gruffly, "What happened here?"

Even though I was totally innocent, I had difficulty staying calm. "Somebody dumped a dead woman."

His lips were thin, as he carefully walked around the corpse. He sighed, "This is serious." He moved a small device over her body and stopped when it beeped. He looked at the device and shook his head slowly as if he couldn't believe the readings.

He sighed when he stood again and asked, "Where were you this morning?"

I was shocked that he dared to ask that question. Clearly he knew I had raised the alarm! But then I realised that I was the only one that used these roads for exercises, and I calmly retorted, "I was training, together with Estrella."

He nodded, "I'm sorry, but I had to ask."

I was somehow relieved when he apologised, and I

said, "No need to apologise. Do you know who she was?"

"Yes, she was one of the best entertaining women in this city. She was highly in demand because of her wide-ranging skills of pleasure."

I was dumbstruck, and before I could ask the obvious question, he said, "She was a professional, and she was the one men went to for really rough sex. But this time I guess it went too far, and she paid with her life for it."

I shivered and said, "It looks more like just a brutal murder to me."

He pondered for a second or two and said, "The autopsy will give us more information, but it looks like she has been killed by a professional."

I said, "I don't understand why she was dumped on the road and not somewhere in the woods."

"To leave a corpse in the woods you need to carry it into the woods which will leave evidence. The body has been dumped on the road from a hover, and it's as if the deceased has appeared from thin air. A lot of men and women will mourn about her. She was a beloved person and besides being a prostitute she did a lot of good for the city."

I felt out of place, and said, "I think I would like to leave now."

As he looked at me, I saw the pain in his eyes when he said, "Of course, I understand. My colleague will take you back. I need to stay here until the research team has arrived."

I walked to the hover and I didn't need to say anything because as soon as I was seated the pilot started the engine. I looked down once more, and I thought I saw the head of security staring at her, shaking a bit as if he was sobbing.

Something was seriously wrong, and I sincerely hoped that this had nothing to do with me choosing to participate in the regeneration ceremony.

I was dropped at the square close to the lunch hall, and

I realised I was in need of a good lunch. When I entered the lunch hall, I was surprised to find out that the death of this woman was already the talk of the day. Everybody who I saw looked shocked and sad. Soon I knew her code name: BB, but nobody knew her real name which kind of made sense as those special ladies were very keen to keep their private life separate from their public affairs.

Estrella joined me fifteen minutes later, and I could see that she had been crying. I didn't dare to ask her about BB, but then she said, "BB was a very good friend. It is a shame that you never met her. You would have liked her."

Not really knowing what to do, I tried to comfort her by holding her hand, and I said, "She was loved by many people."

She took a deep breath and said, "Yes she was. The city won't be the same without her."

There was an eerie silence in the lunch hall, and I felt really uncomfortable. Estrella patted my arm and said a forced smile, "We need to press on. We can't afford to lose much time."

I had finished my lunch, and I said, "Right. I'm ready."

"Okay, back to my quarters. Neither of need any further distractions. Since you're wearing your power suit I know exactly what I'm going to do with you."

Her smile was somewhat mischievous, and I asked playfully, "Oh dear, what are you going to do with me?"

She snickered and said, "Make you sweat."

****

When totally exhausted I arrived at Ellonary's I found the place lit with little lights. Ellonary was lying on her bed curled up in a foetal way. When she looked up to me, I saw her red eyes and I knew she was very upset. I sat down next to her, and she laid her head in my lap and started to sob. I stroked her hair knowing she needed the time to process her loss.

The silence told me that Ellonary was also a close friend of BB. She moved her head and looked up to me. I saw her almond shaped eyes looking at me as if she was pleased I was accepting the situation. She said with a little voice, "Please hug me."

I lay down on my back next to her, and she snuggled up and laid her head on my chest. I kissed her on her hair and asked, "Are you comfortable?"

She nodded, "I am."

After a long moment of silence she sighed, "I'm going to miss her. She was like a mother to me. You could always ask her for advice."

I took her hand, kissed it tenderly and held it while I gently rubbed her fingers. Her breathing started to become more regular and deeper which made me sleepy as well.

I felt relaxed and happy that I could be a help to Ellonary. I was wondering how Estrella would handle the night, and I felt guilty that I was not with her. However, Ellonary's warmth soon lulled me to sleep.

****

The last day that I spent with Estrella was intense and long. Luckily there were no other attempts to end my life or other dead bodies, and I was able to focus on getting ready for the ceremony. It was strange that I wasn't able to concentrate on specific goals, but Estrella was a good teacher. I noticed that Estrella looked for ways to have physical contact with me without focusing on the sexual side. I liked to be close to her, but I was careful not to hurt her even though she tried to engage me in some rough wrestling.

It was the afternoon, and we had been running for a long time. When we arrived at the gardens of the city, she playfully forced me to the ground in a grassy part of the garden. I hadn't expected it, and my initial response was to want to flip her over my shoulder.

She was fast enough to bend her body in such a way that she landed on her feet with a huge grin on her face. She giggled, and I desperately wanted her close by me. I used a trick to lure her to me, moaning as if I was hurt.

Looking concerned she rushed towards me, and when she was close enough, I grabbed her arms and pulled her down next to me. She huffed indignantly but when I kissed her on her lips, her body tensed rigidly.

She whispered urgently, "Xander no! Please don't kiss me in public. It only will bring trouble."

I realised what I had done could be problematic, and I said, "I'm sorry. I didn't think."

Clearly annoyed, she growled, "Why did you wait until the last day to show your affection to me?"

I was unprepared for such an accusatory question but knew that she had a point, and I said softly feeling quite guilty, "I think because you are special, and I wanted to be sure."

Her face softened a bit and said, "You're so silly sometimes. I was on the verge of giving up on you."

I gulped. "I'm sorry."

"Giving up that you would take the first step. Don't you ever think I would have let you go."

I gulped again, and she started to laugh softly. Losing myself in her beautiful eyes, I gently moved a stray strand of hair behind her ear. She said, "Let's get a little to eat before we get changed. I'm ravenous."

****

I was clean, shaven and preparing myself for the last evening together with Estrella. I studied myself closely in the mirror, happy with what I saw. My body had changed completely from a fragile skinny bloke to a Herculean shaped man. I was toned but didn't look too overly trained.

I walked into the bedroom and before I realised it, two

hands covered my eyes while I was gently pulled against two soft breasts. The woman whispered in my ear which I barely could hear, "Be gentle. It's her first time with a man." Then she spoke louder, "Stick your hands out slowly."

I was relieved it was Ellonary who was holding me, and I slowly moved my hands forward quickly coming into contact with two arms.

I carefully moved up to the shoulders and slid down finding out that I was caressing a back. A beeping sound from the ring told that Little Alex was ready for some action. Ellonary had trouble stifling her giggle and gyrated her hips against my behind.

When I reached the small of her back, I moved my hands sideways and pulled her towards me.

I heard a gasp when her bottom touched my hard cock which I quickly readjusted to rest in between her firm cheeks. I slowly stroked her stomach and planted small kisses on her shoulder triggering a trembling sigh.

I knew it was Estrella, and I was in heaven: I was sandwiched between two wonderful women.

I felt Estrella's hands on mine, and she guided me to her breasts. I smiled, incredibly turned on by her impatience deliberately caressing her firm globes slowly avoiding touching her nipples. She whimpered a little and tried to move her torso in such a way as to make me touch them. When I moved my hands away, she moaned even louder and pleaded softly, "Please."

I grabbed her middle, and turned her around to kiss her passionately. Ellonary let go of me, and I was finally able to look straight into Estrella's eyes that were full of desire.

As my hands travelled down to her firm butt, her hands glided over my chest. She smiled and her husky voice made me even hornier when she said, "At last I can touch you. At last, I can be touched by you. Please make me crazy, make me scream your name."

I gently pushed her backwards until she fell on the bed,

and Ellonary gracefully slid next to her.

Her incredible beautiful body was trembling with desire as Ellonary started to kiss her, and I kneeled down to admire her legs by kissing them, inching my way slowly north.

I had to laugh when Estrella grabbed my hair and pulled my face straight between her legs. Her whole body shuddered when I planted a soft kiss right at her hood. Her musky smell made my head turn from desire and I placed a trail of kisses on her hot womanhood.

She moaned as Ellonary moved down to her breasts while I was caressing her silky wetness with my tongue.

I knew it was going to be a fantastic evening.

****

I woke up heavily sweating because I was sandwiched between the two women again. Estrella was against my back, and Ellonary warmed my chest while my rock hard, but very sore member was trapped between her legs.

Last night was incredible, and I was pleased that the two had different wants. Ellonary was good for a rough, hard and fast fuck while Estrella was far more sensual. She wanted to feel everything, going slowly, which was emotionally much more intense.

They complemented each other, and I had never guessed that their intimate friendship would enhance their climaxes.

It felt wonderful being gently squashed between their divine bodies and I dreaded the moment in the next few hours that Estrella had to leave.

Estrella was the first to awake, and while she stretched her body, she kissed me on my neck, snuggling up again by pushing her firm breasts against my back while she stroked my bottom.

Sighing she moved away from me.

I turned around to see what she was doing and was

shocked to see the sad expression on her face.

She perked up instantly and asked, "Will you join me in the shower?"

I smiled, and whispered, "Yes, if only Ellonary will let me."

Giggling softly as she realised the extent of my delicate situation, Estrella carefully crawled over to Ellonary, slowly sliding her hand under Ellonary's foot, she asked softly, "Ready?"

I nodded, relieved to be able to free my privates without any further discomfort. Ellonary moaned softly when Estrella laid her leg down again, but she didn't wake up.

I saw Estrella licking her lips when she noticed my aroused state and her eyes instantly grew a little darker with desire.

As we headed to the bathroom, she asked while pointing at my groin, "Has it been hard all night?"

I chuckled. "Good grief no! It always gets hard in the morning's."

She sighed and said with an apologetic voice, "I don't think I'm up to having you inside me again."

I stroked her cheek, and I said, "Me either. I'm far too sore."

She giggled and confessed, "Me too."

"Let's have a quick shower. Can I still have breakfast with you?"

Her smile was mesmerising as ever, and she said, "Oh yes, I think I can arrange that."

****

After we'd enjoyed a light but filling breakfast, I was taken to a small hall by Estrella where most of the people I knew were gathered.

To my surprise, Ellonary was there, and she looked stunning in her official outfit. She was standing next to the healing master and Layly who also looked exceptional sexy in her dress. It seemed that all the nurses were there, and they all looked very excited.

Estrella who was standing next to me was unable to hide her sadness and I realised that she was afraid that she might never see me again.

I smiled at her, and whispered, "Don't worry. I'll survive the test. I can't let you go just like that."

Taking my hand, she held it for a long moment, squeezing gently as if she didn't want to let go.

We were waiting for the official start of the respite that would be attended by Estrella's mother. There was one other person who was going to do the test as well. He looked like a midget compared to me, and I didn't view him as a threat. I smiled. However, he simply ignored me which I took to be a sign of weakness.

I was surprised to see that the pilot, who had rescued me, was the man's sponsor. His expression was surly, but I gave him a friendly nod anyway. After all he was partly responsible that I was still alive.

A voice shouted, "Attention! Her Highest!"

Estrella let go of my hand, and the people bowed towards the middle of the hall. My rebellious nature caused me to bow a second later than everyone else, but I am not sure that anybody noticed it.

Estrella's mother sounded annoyed when she commanded, "All are spared."

It was the signal that we could stand, and I looked straight at her. I felt sorry for her when I saw the way in which she was dressed. Maybe that was the reason she sounded so depressed.

She stared at me for a second before bestowing an expressionless gaze upon the midget. Her voice which was reflected by the dome, sounded powerful, and her impressive posture made the people in the hall feel small. I was intrigued by the beautiful and carefully crafted place. They were experts at performing magic with just a few simple tricks.

I smiled at Estrella's mother when she looked at me again, and I was surprised that her corner of her lips twisted a little.

Her voice boomed around the hall, "Today two brave men are fighting for the right to enter our society. This choice must genuinely and solely be taken by the individual soul. The time spent during the respite must not be coloured by the sponsor until the regeneration ceremony has started. I wish both men a quiet and restful time, and I hope they will use it wisely."

We bowed to her, as she continued, "If anyone has any objections, then they should speak up now."

There was a moment of silence before the pilot spoke up. "I do, Your Highest."

There was a collective gasp, and it was clear that even Her Highest had not anticipated this. She turned in his direction and asked evenly, "I would like to hear your objection."

He bowed and said with a hoarse voice, "Your Highest. It is written in law that the sponsor is not allowed to share intimate moments with the introduced during the days of respite. I have clear evidence that the introduced had an intimate encounter with his sponsor."

Estrella face turned bright red when her mother looked her and asked with an icy voice, "When was this offence committed?"

The pilot smirked, "Early this morning, Your Highest."

My mind was running at top speed. The bastard had apparently heard our party of three when he passed Ellonary's door! Suddenly I had a thought.

Estrella's mother looked at me with a disappointed expression on her face, "Do you confess to this crime?"

I looked her in the eye when I said, "Your Highest, I have witnesses that can prove that I had breakfast with my sponsor when the large sun showed its first beams. If having breakfast is an intimate encounter then I can assure you that we only discussed this ceremony."

I could see the huge look of relief in her eyes, and a little smile flashed across her lips when she said, "Sponsor, your objection will not be granted. Having breakfast is not seen as an intimate encounter."

She turned to him when he started to sputter, "But Your Highest. They...."

Her voice was deafening when she shouted, "Silence!"

The pilot was clearly affected by the fierce outburst and looked down when she continued, "One more word, and I'll make sure that you and your introduced are sent to the North Quarters."

Estrella shivered when she heard her mother saying the last sentence. I guessed that the North Quarters was a kind of jail in a very cold environment.

Her mother sighed and said with an authoritative voice, "I hereby announce that the respite period has started."

She walked off the platform and looking at us hissed, "Fille, I want you and your introduced in my quarters. Now!"

Estrella replied submissively, "Yes Your Highest, at once."

Grabbing my hand, we rushed out of the hall. I had trouble keeping up with her pace without running. She was clearly concerned, and when I tried to ask her what was wrong, she instantly placed her finger on my mouth and whispered, "Not now. Walls have ears."

I respected her wish, and I followed her without making another sound until we arrived in the big hall with the nice art. She opened a door, and before she went in, she said to me, "Wait here. The head of security will come to get you."

I nodded silently and I gave her an understanding smile.

She quickly closed the door leaving me alone again in the very same hall where we had our first fight. It surprised me that I was able to laugh about it. It seemed so childish compared to the trouble we were in now.

"I've never seen her so angry." a voice behind me commented.

Turning to the familiar face, I said "I've been in more precarious situations before, and survived them all."

His laugh reverberated in the hall, and his face soured in an instant as he said, "We need to hurry. Especially when she is in such a foul mood."

Taking sturdy steps we entered a wonderfully decorated room filled with the most pompous furniture I had ever seen. Estrella was sitting on one of the chairs and bounced up enthusiastically when she saw me.

She waited for the head of security to leave before saying with a somewhat faint smile, "I think we have to be very careful what we are going to say to my mother."

I replied, "Well, I saved our dignity including hers."

Before Estrella could say anything, I heard a snort behind me.

"If you had kept your manhood at bay, this situation wouldn't have occurred."

I turned around to face Estrella's mother who was still in her official dress. She grumbled, "Couldn't you just wait to seduce her after the ceremony?"

This time Estrella shouted, "Mom! It was me who seduced him!"

With tears rolling down her cheeks, she whispered, "Xander is kind, sweet, thoughtful and anything else you would like to find in a man. I wanted to be close to him before he..."

She didn't finish her sentence and stared down to the floor.

I had the urge to hug her, but I didn't dare move closer. There was a long silence, and I heard Estrella's mother sigh while she shook her head. I started to respect her when she said softly, "Xander, thank you for your smart defence at the respite ceremony. It saved us a lot of trouble."

Flabbergasted, I replied, "I'm glad it worked out that way, Your Highest."

She chuckled and said with a stern voice, "I had to use my persuasive powers to keep it all in control."

She was right, and there was no doubt that she had bailed me out of an incredibly difficult situation, "I thank you for that, Your Highest."

She smiled and said with a surprisingly warm voice, "Now, go to the healing master. He will guide you to your inner soul. I wish you good luck."

I never had expected her to change her mind, but it seemed that I had won her heart. I responded genuinely, "Thank you, Your Highest."

I glanced at Estrella before I walked out the room, who was smiling through her tears. When I was halfway down the corridor, I heard Estrella's mother comforting her, "Oh Estrella my dear, I'll do everything in my power to keep him safe."

It gave me a huge boost of confidence hearing those words.

CHAPTER TEN.

As I was walking towards the hall, the head of security joined me and said, "You survived remarkably well."

I was full of confidence and feigned indifference by shrugging, "I guess so."

"Yes, The Highest ordered me to keep you alive at all costs."

I stopped walking, and I asked, "What do you mean?"

He chuckled and started to walk again. He said, "So far, you've been lucky. But maybe you won't be so lucky the next time. I have been tasked with preventing that from happening."

I sighed, and asked, "Do you have any idea why they want me dead?"

He said soberly, "I have a suspicion that the other sponsor doesn't want you to succeed."

I raised my eyebrows and said sarcastically, "Oh really?"

But then I got goose bumps all over me, and I said, "Don't tell me that he is an ex-army."

He seemed impressed by my observation, "He was a highly trained security officer until he fell off a roof and damaged his spine. Even though he has recovered, it would be impossible for him to return to his old position."

Now I was fascinated by his story and I asked eagerly, "Why is that?"

"He failed when he fell which automatically resulted into an honourable dismissal."

I thought for a moment and said, "I assume he was very bitter about that."

There was a silence as if he was thinking if he would reveal such private information to me. He retorted, "Some said that he staged his fall but I think he still hasn't dealt with it and it's backfiring at him at the moment."

That answer intrigued me enormously.

"Why do you think that?" I asked.

"He is getting irrational. Which he wasn't a few cycles ago."

This was very important information for me. I could get killed by this lunatic!

I asked, "How do you know that?"

"Because he is a friend."

"Oh great." I murmured. Why did I end up in such a precarious situation?

He said with a very annoyed voice, "Maybe you should consider that the task given by The Highest is what I *have* to do."

I was taken aback by his response and I realised I forgot who I was talking to. You wouldn't become the head of security just like that. I knew an apology was at its place.

"I didn't think. I'm sorry."

He sighed and kept silent for a moment and then said, "He has changed dramatically and our friendship."

He stopped because when we turned into a corridor the pilot was standing there. He looked different from what he had done earlier this morning. His hair was wet and his face was scratched. He was holding his right hand between his legs as if he has been kicked in his groin.

He had a vile smile when he said hoarsely, "Theodor,

have you become a babysitter now?"

I knew that the pilot had insulted Theodor by addressing him by his name in public but I was more concerned what the pilot had done to get those scratches.

Theodor asked the pilot, "Max, what are you doing here?"

I suddenly realised we were in the corridor where Ellonary lived, and I shouted, "Ellonary!"

His laugh was manic and my adrenaline rushed through my veins. With a roar I pushed him aside and rushed to Ellonary's door. It wasn't shut and I wanted it to push it open but I felt somebody dragging me away.

It was Theodor who snapped, "Careful! There might be a trap."

I realised that the laughing had stopped and when I glanced in that direction I saw that the pilot was lying motionless on the floor. I assumed that Theodor had disabled him in a way but then I realised that it was me who had slammed him against the wall.

Theodor ran his fingers lightly around the doorframe. Looking defeated, he sighed, "There is a trap that I am unable to neutralise. We need to locate Ellonary and then remove her from the situation as quickly as possible. There will be an explosion and there is a risk of contamination from Sweet-Pepper.

"Is there a delay on the trap?"

"Yes, but just a few moments."

"How long will it take before the Sweet-Pepper will ignite?"

"I don't know. It depends on the mixture he has used."

We needed to be protected when rescuing Ellonary. A big sheet of plastic would do the trick.

I said, "I need a big sheet of fabric. You stay under it to get Ellonary and leave it there when you're done."

I saw Theodor's eyes narrowing as he grasped what I had in mind. "That might work if we have an extra person. I'll summon my second to bring the sheet and camera."

Within a minute the corridor was filled with security people and the pilot was taken into custody while still unconscious. I tried calling out to Ellonary but unfortunately she didn't respond and I feared for the worst. It was so frustrating not being able to get to her without triggering the bomb.

Theodor's second in command was to my relief there within five minutes and we quickly moved the camera around the door.

I was shocked when I saw the devastation in the room. Blood was splattered everywhere. We found Ellonary face down on the bed lying in blood stained sheets.

I cursed softly and Theodore said, "Right, My second runs into the room with the sheet and you follow him directly. You pick up Ellonary and get out as fast as possible. Have a good look now where all the debris is lying on the floor to prevent any unnecessary delay."

The sheet had been unfolded and it looked like the plastic was big enough to protect us from the Sweet-Pepper.

I looked at Theodor's second who was holding one end of the sheet above his head and I said, "Thanks for doing this."

He smiled. "Who wouldn't want to rescue Ellonary?"

I was glad he saw it like that and I said, "Okay, I'm ready when you are."

Theodor's second said, "On the count of three. One... two... three!"

He charged into the room with me hot on his heels. We made a tunnel out of the sheet, which protected us and Ellonary. The floor was slippery but we managed to get to her without any unexpected problems. Ellonary's body looked terrible. I could see several stab wounds on her arms and legs, but mercifully he hadn't stabbed her in the back. I saw a pile of blood soaked clothes which I recognised as belonging to the pilot. I was sure the bastard had showered, and dressed in fresh clothes before setting the booby trap.

A deafening bang made my ears ring but the explosion gave me the kick up the backside needed to pick up Ellonary's limp body. As I rushed back to the door I heard the drops of Sweet-Pepper fall on the sheet and I was grateful that we had the foresight to protect ourselves.

I stormed out the apartment only just managing to keep my balance and avoiding crashing into the wall of the corridor.

Bewildered, I looked around for a place where I could bring Ellonary's body in safety. I was grateful to see the healing masters rushing towards me with a stretcher onto which Ellonary was carefully rolled.

Checking her neck for a pulse, one of the masters shouted, "She is still alive."

Her face looked like it had been smashed with a baseball bat. The remains of her ripped tank top were completely drenched with blood. I was shocked to see how badly she had been injured and the hand I was loosely holding looked like it had been trampled on.

They rushed away with the stretcher and I collapsed down on the floor staring at the door to Ellonary's apartment.

I felt the adrenaline rushing through my veins and my heart was pounding like crazy. I have never seen anyone so badly beaten before, and it was all I could do to prevent myself from throwing up.

Theodor came and sat next to me. He patted my leg and said, "You know, if you make it to the end, I want you to offer a position in my team."

I chuckled because I knew he was impressed and I said, "Thanks for the offer. I'll think about it."

He said, "It's best that you are going to stay in the security quarters for the time being."

I nodded, "I think I need a shower and some clean clothes."

We both got up and he chuckled softly before he said,

"I can see that. Follow me, Xander."

The fact that he called me by my name made me feel good. However, all I wanted was to be by Ellonary's side.

****

The water which was running down the drain coloured red when I stepped under the falling water of the shower with my clothes on. I shivered as I recalled her broken body and I had to sit down.

I was grateful for the fact that together with Theodor we had prevented a tragedy. It must be hard for him to be confronted by the fact that his friend was losing it and I wondered what would actually happen to the sad bastard.

After a long while just sitting in the shower I had gained enough energy to get up and I took my wet clothes off so I could wash myself. The unfamiliar smell of the soap which I found in the shower made me speed up.

I was sitting dressed on the bed when I recalled Estrella's plea to her mother. It was clear that Estrella was head over heels in love with me, and I was pleased how her mother responded. She instantly recognised that her daughter was in a difficult situation. I was still trying to get used to the fact that she had been friendly towards me.

A soft knock at the door brought me back to reality and I said with a loud voice "Come in. Door is open."

Theodor's second man entered the room and he asked, "All okay?"

I nodded, "Yes, considering the circumstances."

He grinned and said, "Geldor."

"Sorry?"

He repeated, "Geldor. My name is Geldor."

I smiled, "Xander, but I guess you knew already."

"Yes I did. I was asked to escort you to your healing master."

I was eager to go because I was curious what the healing master had prepared for me and I said, "I think I can use some guidance after what I have witnessed today."

He sighed, "Yes, It was shocking to see Ellonary like that."

I couldn't help but feel jealous.

I stared at him with a somewhat strained questioning look and he explained, "We liked to hunt together. I taught her to shoot at moving objects."

I laughed with relief and I said, "You have done an excellent job. I'm standing here because she managed to kill an Anix when it attacked me."

As we walked out the door he said enthusiastically, "That's my girl! I'm proud of her."

It was really hard to determine Geldor's age but I guessed he was a lot older than me. I sighed and I said, "I really hope that she will recover fully."

He patted me on my back, "She will be fine and because of your brilliant plan she doesn't have any Sweet-Pepper burns."

I shivered, "I really hate that stuff."

"Tell me about it." He pulled his sleeve up and showed me an ugly scar on his arm and said, "This is what happens if Sweet-Pepper lands on your skin."

"That looks really nasty."

He pulled his sleeve back down and said placidly, "It took about four seasons to fully heal."

We walked in silence to the healing master's office, pondering about the day's events. As we neared, he said, "I want to give you a hint: let it all be. Forget the strangeness and use the benefit of the guidance."

I saw his smile which reached his eyes and I said, "Thanks, I appreciate it." I was becoming more and more intrigued about what the healing master had prepared for me.

As he walked away he said, "Good luck Xander."

I turned to knock at the door but before I could raise my hand the door was opened by the healing master.

He said sounding very friendly, "Enter my boy. Do

enter."

I didn't recognise his office at all. It was completely changed and a strange smelling scent was burning on top of a small table which was situated in the middle of the total empty room.

The light was low and had a dark orange glow.

He indicated that I should sit on a mattress that was next to the table.

The wrinkles round his eyes looked much deeper when he smiled and he said, "Before we start I want to tell you that Ellonary will recover completely."

I sighed, feeling incredibly relieved. "Thank you healing master. I needed that to hear."

He chuckled and put a hand on my shoulder. "She is an incredibly strong woman. Now, I'm afraid we need to squeeze the program a bit to recover the lost time. Normally I would explain what we are going to do. So lie down and listen to my voice and try to relax."

I lay down on the mattress and did as he asked.

CHAPTER ELEVEN.

I woke up, feeling really strange as if my body had been cast in concrete. I was able to open my eyes a little but was unable to see anything other than the orange coloured ceiling of the room I was in. I was extremely groggy and was unable to recall much about recent events. I must have been given a drug that had clearly had a powerful effect on me.

The door opened very slowly, which was unusual. I sensed that someone was checking up on me but had no idea as to their intentions.

Because of recent events I was prepared for everything and I pretended that I was still out even though I felt a panic rising in my body. Peeking through my eyelashes, it took every ounce of willpower that I possessed to remain calm, as I had to wait for whoever it was to come into my field of vision.

It had seemed like ages before I saw a female carefully tiptoeing towards the head of the mattress. I had an amazing view of her legs because she was wearing a skirt. Crossing her legs she stood there for at least five minutes looking at me. I heard a soft sigh and then she lifted her skirt to get something from her garter belt. She dropped her skirt again and a moment later she started to walk slowly around the mattress. I was certain that I heard little drops falling on the fabric of the mattress.

Sensing danger all around me, I was desperate to get away but wasn't even able to move my fingers! Much as I tried, I was unable to tense any of my muscles and it was pure torture trying to keep my breathing even as if I was fast asleep. I couldn't see her, but heard a rustling of her skirt as she hid the little bottle. A few beeps and the door slid open. When the door was closed, I heard her walking away and I was pretty sure I heard the familiar sound of high heels.

I was lying there absolutely unable to move a single muscle and this time I definitely could smell the soothing sweet odour.

Sweet-Pepper!

My heart was racing as I felt a slight tingle in my hand, and I managed to move my fingers a bit. I knew I had to move them to get my blood flowing to get rid of the toxins. Realising that I was also able to move my toes, I started to wriggle them frantically.

The sweet smell was getting even stronger, and I knew that the chemical reaction had started to warm up the places where the fluid had drenched the fabric.

Pleased that I was at least able to move my wrists and ankles, I was dismayed by the fact that my arms and legs felt numb. Luckily I could breathe deeper and I started to pump my lungs with air trying to get the toxins out of my body.

The sweet smell had already been replaced by a nasty acrid smell that made me sweat because it felt as if I was still nailed to the mattress.

I knew it was a race against the chemical reaction as to whether or not I would be able to get away on time. Taking deep breaths, I sucked in air, only to be thwarted by the stench of the smouldering fabric that caught in the back of my throat making me cough. Ironically the coughing turned out to be my saviour as it forced me to sit up.

With an enormous effort, I pushed myself up off the mattress doing my best to avoid the dark patches that were clearly visible.

Stumbling to the door, I was surprised when it opened normally. A quick glance down the corridor told me that nobody was there and I decided to head straight to my own place as no one would think to look there for me right now. The fresh air helped enormously and within no time I was able to walk normally again. Furious, doesn't begin to cover it! It was hard to believe that someone would deliberately drench the mattress with Sweet-Pepper!

Back in my room, I got undressed and dived into the shower in an attempt to relax my extremely stiff and tense muscles. I needed to think about what I wanted to do.

The fact that my would-be killer was a woman gave me cause for thought. I was seriously starting to think that leaving the planet was the best thing to do. Within a minute, I had formulated a plan that would ensure my safety until the regeneration ceremony. I jumped out of the shower and quickly dried myself before rushing to the communications device that was hanging on the wall. By now the mattress should have been burning for a while, and the authorities would have been alerted. I touched the screen, and a synthesised voice asked, "Who do you want to connect to?"

"Theodor, head of security of The Highest. It's a high priority matter. "

"One moment please, trying to connect."

Suddenly Theodor's voice sounded agitated through the speaker, "This had better be good!"

I said, "It's Xander."

I heard shouting and loud pounding against something while I waited for him to respond. I knew that they were breaking down the door to the healing master's office and I guessed that the unknown woman had changed the settings on the door.

He sighed and said, "By Yourian, where are you?"

"I'm at my own place. I left the healing master's place because a woman managed to drench the mattress with Sweet-Pepper."

He ordered, "Describe the woman."

"High heels, skirt, blond hair, braided."

"High heels?"

"Yes, the shoes were raised at the back."

"Oh heel pushers. Do you remember the colour of the skirt?"

"It was too dark but I think it was a dark colour."

I heard a loud cracking sound and a lot of shouting afterwards. I assumed that they had managed to force the door.

Theodor said, "I guess I found her."

My heart was pounding with excitement and I was wondering if there was anything else that might be of use to Theodor.

I remembered the little scene when she was standing close to my head and I said, "Oh wait Theodor! She lifted her skirt. I guess she is hiding the Sweet-Pepper there."

Theodor said, "Great. Thanks. Stay where you are. I'll pick you up later."

He hung up before I could respond to his request and I felt more at ease even though I was desperate for him to capture the woman who had attempted to kill me.

I went back to the bathroom to get dressed.

It felt like an eternity before there was a knock at the door.

I asked, "Who's there?"

A man answered, "Someone who doesn't wear high heels."

I opened the door with a grin and let Theodor in.

He quickly shut it and gestured me to sit down on the bed.

I looked at him with anticipation and asked, "Any

luck?"

He sighed and said darkly, "Yes and I'm sure you're not going to like it."

"Oh?"

"It was nurse Layly."

"No! I can't believe that!"

"She had a little flask with Sweet-Pepper attached to her garter. She believes you to be dead as do most people. However, I told Estrella and her mother that you're fine."

I was shocked. Layly had been really nice to me and I didn't understand why she had done it.

Theodor saw my face and he said, "She was jealous."

"Ellonary." I responded with a sigh.

"Yes, she complained about not getting enough attention from you and she got the Sweet-Pepper from Max."

Thinking back to the moments when I was with her I was now able to see that the clues had been there all along. It was her lingering and the little tremble in her hands and the way she fell silent when I told her I wanted to wash myself. I thought she had taken it light-heartedly but presumably I was wrong. Now because I hadn't noticed her dismay she had set fire to the healing master's office.

I looked down at the floor, furious at myself for messing up their world. My presence had caused a huge upset and created an imbalance.

I whispered, "I think it is better that I leave your planet. I have caused only discomfort and upset."

He laughed and after a while he said, "Yes, you did mess up our daily life but I assure you it was starting to become extremely indolent."

I wasn't sure what he was talking about and I asked, "What do you mean?"

"Everything is neatly organised and nothing really happened until you came on to our world. It's so funny that you were Estrella's first and last assignment."

I was intrigued and I instantly asked, "What kind of

assignment are you talking about?"

Theodor suddenly looked a lot paler and said, "Oh. Err, I'm sorry. I can't tell you that. I've said too much already. I'm sorry."

I liked him and I knew that he couldn't say more so I said, "Never mind. I probably won't survive the test anyway."

He smiled, "I wouldn't count on that. You aren't the average person."

I was thinking about the fact that my death was staged and I asked, "How am I going to do the test? I am supposed to be dead."

"We'll keep you hidden until the regeneration ceremony."

"How about the respite?"

He paced around my room and said, "I don't want to risk letting anyone else in on our secret. I'm afraid you will have to do with whatever you have learned from the healing master today."

I sighed; two full days in solitude. I knew I had to accept my destiny and lay low for the time being.

****

I was lying on my bed fretting over what had happened over the course of the last few days. Survival on this planet had already proven to be a huge challenge. I was worried that because I was missing the respite treatment I would miss a vital part of my survival training.

I heard a soft knock at the door and a familiar sounding female voice said, "I'm wearing high heels."

I grinned; amused by the fact that Theodor had instructed her to use this specific phrase.

I opened the door but couldn't make out who was entering my room because the woman's black cloak was hiding her face.

My heart skipped a beat as the cloak slipped gracefully

to the floor. I had followed the fall of the cloak and when I slowly looked up I saw an incredible sexy and voluptuous body dressed in sweat pants and a tight-fitting tank top.

Her legs were not completely visible but they had a nice curve which ended into her wide hips. Her stomach was not completely flat but it flowed wonderfully to her full breasts.

My mouth was agape as I stared into the blue grey eyes of Estrella's mother. She looked a lot younger and her black hair was tied up into a ponytail.

She chuckled nervously and said after a moment, "I'm flattered by your reaction but you can close your mouth now."

She tossed a bag on the bed and said, "Here are some clean clothes. Maybe you should wear something suitable for a serious stretch session."

Realising that I was in my briefs, my face turned bright red. She smiled warmly and said with a calm voice, "You have a wonderfully toned body but I don't think you have been stretching those muscles enough."

I picked up the bag and rushed into the bathroom while I said hoarsely, "I'll be back in a few moments."

I had never dressed myself that quickly and when I came back in the room she had moved some of the furniture to create more space in front of the bed.

I sat down on my bed and I asked, "Your Highest why are you here?"

She sat next to me and smirked before commanding, "Stop calling me Your Highest. Use Laura for now."

I couldn't believe what she had just had said but her amazing looking body was very close to me and I was spellbound.

I said in a whisper, "I'm honoured to know your beautiful name Laura, but why are you doing this?"

She sighed, "I had hoped you were smarter. I'm going to be your guide for the rest of the respite."

I was very happy and amazed that she wanted to do

that. I was puzzled as to the reasons why she had chosen to guide me but I was afraid to ask her again so I said, "That is very kind of you. I was just preparing myself to have to survive two extremely dull days."

She muttered, "I'm not sure if you will still like me when we are done, but I assure you that our time together won't be dull."

I looked at her and I said genuinely, "Anything you do to help me to prepare for the regeneration ceremony, I'll take as a gift."

Her cloak was spread out on the floor and to my surprise it was inflated so we could use it as a practice matt.

She commanded with a soft voice, "Enough talk. I want to see some action. Lie down on the mat on your back and raise your legs in the air."

****

Her schedule was punishing, and after I had undertaken a series of stretches and push-ups, Laura looked at me thoughtfully,

"I think you need some extra weight. It looks like it's far too easy for you. Keep your body away from the mat."

I complied and kept my body hovering just above the mat. I was completely flabbergasted when she moved towards me and sat slowly on my back. She acted as if it was something completely normal to do and said with an impatient voice, "Go on, let those muscles work!"

I started to do the push-ups again and her weight made it more difficult but I still had enough power to do the exercise.

Suddenly I had the urge to show off how much power I had and I pushed up with such a speed that she nearly tumbled off my back.

She grunted and said, "Right, mister smart. Stop."

I chuckled and I stopped. I really liked the way she was

trying to make the exercise more demanding.

She got up from my back and before I realised what was happening I felt two arms around my chest.

She was lying on top of me and she commanded, "Try again but I want you to move twice as fast."

I started to push up again, this time slowly increasing the speed. It worked out okay in the beginning, but the very fact that she was lying on my back was problematic for me. She pressed her arms tighter around my chest and I started to feel her breasts pressing against my back, but was most aroused by the fact that her pubic bone was pounding against my bottom. As I kept on going my cock was steadily growing to its full length and the ring, which I was still wearing around my member, beeped.

I heard Laura gasp.

She yelled, "Xander! Stop!"

I instantly stopped and she tumbled of me on the mat. Looking as though she had seen a ghost she hissed, "Go to the bathroom and take that ring off instantly! Try to cool down while I get some extra tools for our practice."

As I scrambled to the bathroom I heard Laura taking the cloak from the floor and she rushed out.

I was dumbstruck and I looked at the ring around my trembling shaft. I turned the ring counter clock wise and it instantly increased in size. I took it off and I inspected it closely and I came to the conclusion it was the most sophisticated tool I ever had seen.

This world was strange and the people who inhabited it were even stranger. I hadn't a clue why I had to remove the ring. It was such a wonderful device and it was definitely better than a condom.

I splashed my face with cold water trying to cool down. I had never seen Laura so shocked and I didn't understand what I had done.

The knock at the door brought me back to reality and I reluctantly opened it to face Laura after our embarrassing encounter.

She was carrying a package which she placed next to the door. She sat down on the bed and patted it gesturing me to sit next to her. She took a deep breath before she said softly, "As I am The Highest I'm not allowed to get pregnant. It would result in my death and the death of the male who made me pregnant."

She sighed and said, "You are extremely attractive but we need to keep our relationship at a professional level. Knowing that you don't wear a ring will remind me of my status."

I didn't buy her story but it was clear that we couldn't have sex. I doubted the ethics of a man having a relationship with both a mother and her daughter, and I was pleased that we were at least in agreement about that.

I said trying to move the conversation away from the delicate situation, "Okay that's clear. What did you bring with you?"

Her face lit up into an evil grin as she said, "Your nightmare."

The package was indeed my worst nightmare: It was a special jacket that I had to wear. I was absolutely flabbergasted when I suddenly felt the jacket become heavier.

With a cunning smile Laura showed me the remote control where she was able to increase the weight of the jacket with a simple turn of a dial.

****

I was lying on my stomach in bed feeling much better than I had two days earlier. It had been the most intense and strenuous days of my life. Laura definitely knew how to squeeze that last bit of power out of my body. I had to admit that at no time did I want it to stop.

I'm sure she enjoyed those two days as much as I did and her genuine laugh was contagious.

At the end of the first day I got the impression that she

was loosening up a bit. On the last night, when her task was complete, she hugged me for a long time and whispered in my ear, "Thank you for the wonderful time Xander. I'm going to remember this for a long time."

When I looked in her eyes a little tear ran down her cheek which I gently rubbed away and I said, "Thank you for being so patient. I'm going to miss calling you Laura."

She chuckled and as she walked out the room she said, "If I'm not in those hideous clothes you can use my name Xander. Now rest. Tomorrow will be a long and tiring day."

I sighed and I turned on my back knowing I had to get up soon. When I opened my eyes I saw Estrella sitting next to me with a warm smile. She whispered, "Hi."

My voice croaked a bit when I said, "Hi back."

She slid her body next to mine and said, "I've missed you."

I rubbed her back softly and I replied, "Me too."

I suddenly remembered the wonderful time we had shared with Ellonary and I asked, "How is Ellonary doing?"

She said with a little tremor, "She is healing fast. They will wake her up this afternoon. We will have a few moments with her alone."

I asked, "How much time do we have before we have to go?"

She kissed me softly and said regrettably, "It is time to get ready Xander. Theodor will be here soon."

I got up and when I came back from the bathroom Estrella said, "I don't know what you have done to her but my mother has changed."

I responded, "Uh oh."

She giggled. "Don't be so stupid. You made her happy and she is smiling again. Thank you Xander."

I chuckled and I said, "I think you mother loves to torment young guys. She's had her fix now."

She scowled, "Not funny. Put these clothes on will

you?"

I suddenly had the urge to kiss her and I took her face between my hands. I said, "I will Estrella because you asked it so nicely," and I planted a tender kiss on her lips.

She giggled against my lips and slapped my butt.

I looked at the clothes which were lying on the bed and I decided to wear them because they didn't look that bad at all.

I was zipping up the shoes when Theodor arrived at my place. He inspected my clothes and smiled when he said, "Right, we will have breakfast with Laura and after that you and Estrella will have time to prepare for the ceremony."

Estrella looked at me with a wide grin when she said, "I know exactly how I'm going to prepare you."

I felt a tingle in my groin when I saw the burning lust in her eyes and I huskily joked, "I wonder what that would be."

Theodor raised one eyebrow and asked, "Are we ready?"

In unison we agreed, "Yes."

****

I paced nervously around the small room where we had been told to wait before we could visit Ellonary. Estrella had a healthy glow on her cheeks following our incredibly intense "preparation" for the regeneration ceremony. I blame it on the fact that I haven't had sex for the last three days. We had to improvise a bit though because I no longer had the ring. However, it was still incredibly satisfying for both of us.

The door opened and the healing master came in. He shook my hand and said, "Xander, I'm so pleased you didn't die a horrible death."

His clumsy remark made me chuckle inwardly. However, I knew that he meant well. I replied sarcastically,

"Yes, who knows how I will die at the ceremony."

He looked shocked at me and said, "I'm sorry. I was not thinking."

I said, "It's okay. How is Ellonary?"

He perked up a little and said, "She is awake and has asked for you both."

I grabbed Estrella's hand and I walked out the room while I said, "What are we waiting for. Where is she?"

The healing master spoke a bit louder, "Take the second door on your left."

I slowly opened the door expecting to see Ellonary surrounded by all kinds of equipment but there was just the bed that she was lying in.

Her face still had some marks and bruises but she looked fantastic compared to the moment I laid her out on the stretcher. She had a painful smile on her face and said with a croaky voice, "My hero, my lovely Xander."

Estrella squeezed my hand when I said, "I couldn't have done it without Geldor and Theodor."

Ellonary said while slowly raising her arms, "Hug me. I want to feel your warm body."

I gently hugged her as I felt her sobbing.

When I let her go I saw that her face was red from the tears and I said, "Hey, don't cry. I'll be back."

Estrella was holding her hand when Ellonary said, "Thank you for saving my life Xander."

I knew that if it wasn't for Theodor's incredible speed that she would otherwise have been in a far worse situation and I said softly, "You're welcome."

She sighed and closed her eyes for a moment. When she opened her eyes again I saw a raw fiery look on her face and she said, "Don't you dare fail at the ceremony. I want to enjoy your divine body as soon as possible."

We all laughed but it quickly died down and I said, "A lot has happened and I'm sure Estrella will fill you in with all the gory details. Thankfully, Estrella's mother has personally been training me, so I am more confident in my ability to survive."

Ellonary gasped and started coughing but her eyes showed that she got the joke. As she was calmed down she said hoarsely, "Poor you. I hope you didn't suffer too much."

Estrella shouted with a laugh, "Ellonary!"

I kissed Ellonary once more on her lips and struggled to control myself. I wanted to know one thing before I left her and I asked, "Ellonary, where did you get the name Sweet-Pepper?"

She was looking a bit puzzled and then she frowned while she growled, "It was Max who called me that, but I thought it fitted you better."

I smiled with relief, "I knew I was sweet."

Estrella punched me on the arm and scowled, "Don't start to be bombastic."

The healing master entered the room and said in a friendly tone, "I know you want to stay longer but it is time."

I gave Ellonary a quick kiss on her lips while she desperately hugged me and I said, "Hang on there."

She whispered, "I will Xander. Keep Estrella and me in your heart."

CHAPTER TWELVE.

Ellonary being so emotional upset me. I knew that she was going to need a lot of TLC before feeling herself again. Everything was going so fast that I hadn't had the time to think properly about events as they rolled out before me.

Now I was standing opposite the midget on a platform next to a hover. At the platform was a large arrow which pointed at an angle to the air. The floor had several rings of different colours and the shadow of the arrow's point was nearly in the middle circle. I assumed it was an ancient time device.

The midget had a new sponsor who was nervously looking around and suddenly ducked down to whisper something in the midget's ear. I couldn't hear what he was saying but it was clear that he didn't like what was going on.

Everyone immediately bowed when someone shouted, "The Highest!"

Like always Laura strode onto the platform completely dressed in the pompous clothes. I noticed that her makeup was less exaggerated which made her face look much more sophisticated and she seemed more relaxed. I was absolutely gobsmacked by the fact she had taken my remarks seriously when we had our animated conversation about her hideous makeup.

She saw that I looked at her with a wide grin.

She gave me a warm smile and winked before speaking, "All be spared."

I smiled at her when her voice boomed over our heads, "It is the first day of a new lunar. A new beginning and for the introduced, a new start. They will find themselves in a new adventure, a new challenge. If they are brave enough they will survive. We will cherish their aid towards the challenge and we will welcome them back with open arms."

A cheer erupted from the people surrounding the platform.

I looked around and saw Estrella who was standing next to the healing master. When she noticed I was looking at her, she blew me a kiss and I winked back at her.

Laura continued, "As described in the ancient laws their challenge will start as soon as the shadow reaches the inner circle."

She addressed us and said, "Introduced. Will the spirits spare you and I wish you good luck."

I bowed to her and I said, "Thank you, Your Highest."

The midget's voice was remarkably low and rumbled with a very strange accent, "Thank you, Your Highest."

The two security men who were standing next to the hover nodded which was the signal to us to get in the hover.

It was a bigger hover than the ones I have seen before and there was no hatch. There was a row of seats mounted at the back wall of the hover but I decided not to sit down.

Together with the pilot we were the only ones at the hover. The pilot turned his chair and said, "It will be a smooth trip until the mountains. It might be bumpy there depending upon how many storm clouds have been formed. I will not land so you will have to jump the last few feet. I wish you good luck."

He turned back to the controls and the hover started to make more noise. I felt a little tremble when the hover started to lift up in the air and I looked out to the crowd. I thought it was very strange that nobody waved. I wondered how much of my previous life was starting to seep through because I knew for sure that people would have waved back home.

I looked out for bit longer but the height and the fact that I wasn't alone made me take a step back from the opening. I turned around and I suddenly felt a sharp pain in my upper arm.

I grunted from the pain and when I looked up, I stared into a knife.

The pain was excruciating and I realised that my other hand was covering the wound. I had to concentrate really hard to get my focus back to dull the pain. I knew I could do it but I had never had another opportunity to practice it and the pain had never been this severe. I managed to dull the pain a bit more and stop my heart from pounding..

The wide grin on his face made him even more gruesome than he was and he said in his strange accent, "This is where your trip ends."

I couldn't believe that he managed to smuggle the knife on board. We had been searched before entering the platform. After that we were given our stick which had been laid on the seats when we had entered the hover. His sponsor must have slipped him the knife when bowing to whisper to him.

I moved slowly away from the opening and I asked with a very calm voice, "Why is that?"

He scolded angrily, "It's because of you that I lost Max as my sponsor."

I managed to numb out the pain completely and I was surprised that the wound stopped bleeding as well. I sighed and said, "What did you expect? He is a murderer!" As we spoke, I took tiny steps towards the middle of the hover.

His horrible grin appeared on his face again when he growled, "Oh her. She was not nice to me and so she had to suffer."

I was starting to lose my temper and I asked, "Did you hurt her?"

"No, Max did."

I snorted and said, "You're a weak person; letting others do the real stuff."

He shouted, "Shut up! You don't even know what I've done on this stupid planet!"

I noticed that there was dried up blood on the knife as well and I knew that he was the one who had killed BB. I sneered, "I see that you like to kill women as well."

His face became red as he spat, "She was stupid not to give in. She never screamed even when I truly hurt her. She had to die!"

I had heard enough and I said, "You're too weak. You don't even dare to hurt me with that pathetic little knife when you look at me."

That did the trick and he charged at me with a howling roar.

I moved my body with ease out of the trajectory of his knife by turning sideways but then realised that I had made a terrible mistake.

The midget charged straight at the pilot's neck!

With horror I saw the knife slide with a sickening crunch into the pilot's head.

The midget charged so fast that he flipped over the pilot's chair and landed at the controls of the hover.

I felt the hover rolling sharply but before I could grab something to hold on I fell through the opening and out of the hover.

As I was freefalling my mind did the most bizarre thing: I saw everything in slow motion which gave me time to act. I saw tree tops coming towards me and I desperately tried to get hold of one but because of the blood on my hand, it was slippery.

I finally managed to grab hold of a very thin and long tree top in my hands just long enough to slow my fall. At the moment the top was about to snap I was able to grab another tree top with my other hand.

The pain flared up but it was not as severe as I thought it would be. I quickly swapped hands and in the end I was dangling about a few feet away from a sturdy branch of a large tree.

While I was dangling I heard an explosion which was a few miles away. The hover must have crashed and I felt sorry for the pilot but I was hoping that the midget was still in there when it happened.

I let myself go and I landed on the sturdy branch which immediately started to groan because of my weight. It quickly lost its sturdiness and I tried to run towards the trunk but I was too late.

With a loud crack I tumbled down together with the branch and braced myself for the inevitable impact.

With a smack I fell on the spongy ground and I was fine until the branch hit my head. I saw stars for a moment and I cursed heavily while I was rubbing the painful place on my head. I nearly forgot about my ability to dull the pain and I took a deep breath to regain my focus on the painful place. I closed my eyes to shut out all other distractions and I addressed both places where I felt the pain. My arm was throbbing but I could deal with it and the pain in my head was different but I felt the level of pain going down rapidly.

When the pain had subsided I looked around the forest to see if there were any signs of civilisation. I saw a lighter part which looked like an open space and I was hoping it would have a path.

I struggled through the dense part of the forest and when I arrived at the open space I knew I was lucky. There was evidence of a fairly recently burned fire and there was a path.

I was certain there was a place close by where people would live and feeling positive I started to follow the path. The path led away from the crashed hover but if they needed directions to find the hover I could direct them from this place.

I was happy that the path was used often because it made my trip a lot easier and after a fifteen minutes' walk I ended up near a fast running river. It was running too fast to cross and it was too wide to jump to the other side.

As I was looking around, to my surprise I saw a bunch of long sticks neatly lying next to the riverbank. I checked the sticks but most of them were too thin. There were just two sticks which might be strong enough to hold my weight and they clearly weren't used as much as the thinner ones.

I checked them both before opting for the thickest one. I looked at the river which was about twelve feet wide and I poked the riverbed with my stick. There was a place which was not as deep as the rest and I knew I had to aim my stick there. I tested the riverbed once more to convince myself that I had a chance of successfully crossing the river.

I took several deep breaths and I walked a few feet away. Charging forward, I managed to place the stick at a perfect spot. With a graceful bow I landed a few feet away from the water and I was actually impressed by how strong that old piece of wood apparently was.

I saw a similar bunch of sticks stacked at this side of the river and I placed my stick on the pile. I looked around to see if there were more paths but there were no others as far I could see.

I continued following the path knowing I would reach civilisation at some time all the while hoping and praying that I would do so before dark and without bumping into another Anix.

The path was windy and the vegetation next to the path was starting to get thicker. It felt like I was walking in a maze, unable to look beyond the path.

Without warning, I heard a snapping noise as if someone had trampled on a branch. I stopped instantly listening intensely for further sounds. I looked up to see if there was movement in the trees but I couldn't see anything that resembled danger. I slowly moved forward trying not to make any noise.

I heard a popping noise and an instant later felt a sting in my neck. As I tried to reach for the back of my neck, I knew that I had failed.

It was then that I heard the choir of voices and the blackness surrounded me.

****

I woke up feeling something soft caressing my back. I was still very groggy and I really enjoyed the soft hands moving very slowly over my body. I started to realise that I hardly could move but the pleasure of the caressing overruled my common sense.

I couldn't discern how many hands were stroking me but I felt my skin tingling wonderfully all over. Some of the hands were starting to get bolder and moved closer to my groin. I knew that my aroused state would be soon discovered. The hands didn't hesitate when they found my throbbing member and a few started to stroke it even slower than the other hands on my skin.

My head wasn't clear and I felt numb as if I was drugged but this allowed me to enjoy the slow but steaming hot caressing of my body. I felt warm bodies lying against me, moving with the same rhythm as the hands. My body was stirred up into the heated rhythm but I was beginning to lose all coherent thought. I gently sailed away into an arousing darkness.

****

I felt warm and relaxed when I came to and I heard a female voice saying, "He is different."

A more mature voice replied, "He is, and much stronger."

"It seems like that our sisters were....connected."

The older voice chuckled. "Yes, I could feel the raw energy flowing. He is special. Special enough to investigate. Prepare him."

"Yes Elder, I'll see to it."

A few moments later I heard the scary choir of voices again and the horrible blackness took over.

****

I found myself lying on my back and tied to a hard surface when I came to. My arms and legs were spread out wide and my chest felt constricted. My head was clear and I was pleased that the groggy feeling had completely vanished.

I had to think hard what had happened. I knew I had been hit, most probably by a poisoned arrow and that they had moved me to this place. It was dark but I could still see the contours of the room where I was and when I looked around I realised that I wasn't alone. I asked, "Why am I tied down like this?"

It was the same mature voice that I had heard before who said, "It's for your own safety."

"What are you going to do with me?"

She got up and walked towards me but it was too dark to see her face. She moved behind my head and I flinched when I felt her cold hand touching my forehead. My skin started to tingle where she held her hand and my vision enhanced enormously.

I suddenly saw that the whole room was filled with small naked female creatures that looked like human apart from their deep, red skin. Their long hair, almond shaped eyes, small lips, sharp looking nails were as black as the nipples on their perky breasts which made them look like little sexy devils. They all were looking at me with a strange dreamy expression on their faces.

The woman said, "They feel what you feel which has never happened before. They are connected to you via a very special bond. Do you know why that might be?"

I felt the warmth of the creatures and I had the impression that they were very familiar. I asked, "What are they?"

"They are the Garntuoas."

I gasped and all the Garntuoas reacted as well by moaning softly.

The woman sneered, "Tell me! Why did you react like that?"

I was still taken aback by the reaction of the red creatures and stammered, "My, my nerve system has been replaced with Garntuoa nerves."

Her voice resounded in the room, "No! No! How dare they send you here!"

I didn't understand why she was so angry and I asked with a soft voice, "What is wrong?"

She moaned, "The blood line. We have ruined the blood line."

I felt guilty and all the red females crawled towards me as if something had triggered them. I quickly counted them, and deduced that there were twelve pairs of hands stroking my naked body.

While they were stroking me I was surprised by the images I could see. They projected images of two other pregnant Garntuoas. I whispered incredulously, "You have used my seed."

The woman replied clearly surprised, "They can communicate with you!" She took a deep breath before she continued, "Yes, you see, every person brought to us has given us a part for the ultimate combination of genes we have been carefully creating for many periods. Now with your contaminated sperm we have lost our precious gene chain."

I was not completely sure why my seed could be changed but I got an image from the little females which showed my seed to be coloured red as they were and I said, "My body has changed a lot more than just my nerves."

She sighed and said with a desolate voice, "Yes, you are now more Garntuoa than human."

It would have shocked me if I hadn't had my own doubts already as to whether I was just a normal guy with Garntuoa nerves. I felt a little betrayed with the result that a few red soft bodies snuggled up to me. It really made me feel better and I was wondering how I could help to solve this problem. A moment later I got an array of images. The first one was about one of the Garntuoas who was pregnant with Estrella. The next few images were about Estrella growing bigger and becoming a woman. The last image was of Estrella being pregnant with my seed and I said flabbergasted, "Estrella!"

The woman who was still behind me asked, "What do you mean?"

I didn't want to answer directly and I asked, "Why is it so important to have the right genes?"

"Because we nearly exterminated the Garntuoa. There are only thirty Garntuoas left but they can't have any male offspring. We, the Youriens, were at war with them and we used the most horrible weapon ever created against them. It killed all the male Garntuoas and the DNA was completely altered. If we have composed the right gene pool combination the Garntuoas will be able to bear males again."

I suddenly understood why this was so important and I knew I had no other choice but to relay the information. I said, "A male child conceived by me and Estrella will save the blood line."

It also explained my strong urge to be with Estrella all the time and I couldn't believe how excited I became at the thought of creating life. I suddenly felt loved by all the Garntuoas and one of them bit me on my neck. Her little teeth sank into my skin and I was lost in a warm darkness.

CHAPTER THIRTEEN.

I woke up slowly and I kept my eyes closed because I wanted to sleep longer. I was lying on my side with a bandage around my arm. I concentrated on the cut and it felt as if it was nearly healed. Slowly I started to awaken and become more aware of my environment.

I knew I was lying in a bed and I felt a warm body lying against my back. I turned around very slowly to find one of the Garntuoas lying there fast asleep. Her black hair was spread over her pillow and she looked incredibly beautiful. Her small black shiny lips, high cheek bones, long eyelashes and elegant eyebrows made her look like a goddess. Her red skin had a terracotta tint which was flawless as far as I could see.

As I was admiring her she stretched her toned body and when she opened her eyes, a dazzling smile appeared on her face. She touched my skin with her hand and I got a picture of her being happy. She snuggled up closer and when we touched skin to skin it felt as was if we were one. She showed that we shared the same nerves and she knew that she had saved my life which made her feel honoured.

She hugged me tighter and kissed my neck softly. I was getting extremely aroused when I felt her perky breasts pressing against my chest. She looked at me with a naughty smile and sent me a row of pictures.

We couldn't make love in the same way that I could do with Estrella because her vagina was simply too small to accommodate the size of my dick. But because we had the same nerves we could experience each other's orgasm and she was looking forward to do that again.

I vaguely remembered having an orgasm which she confirmed by showing me a very erotic picture; I was surrounded by several Garntuoas while on the verge of having an orgasm.

I stroked her back and received a picture of her round and firm bottom. I chuckled when I saw that she pouted when I didn't comply immediately.

She moaned softly and closed her eyes when I gently caressed her unbelievably soft bottom. In an instant I was overwhelmed by her emotions and I felt what my hand was doing on her skin! I shuddered with desire and I knew that I wanted to go slow to enjoy every single moment.

She kissed me softly on my lips while showing me images warning me that I had to be careful with her saliva and other bodily fluids as they would make me drowsy which would spoil the fun.

I thought I would enjoy stroking her and she giggled when I moved my lips down to the swell of her breasts. She gasped when I gently nibbled on her nipple which instantly changed into a protruding black berry. She was clearly overwhelmed because I lost our connection and I hugged her gently trying to comfort her. She showed me I had to be very gentle because she was still sore of the last session.

Meanwhile she had captured my throbbing member between her legs which was a very pleasant feeling. She asked if she could stroke it with her hands.

As I turned on my back she moved sensually to my groin and she brought her hips forward while caressing my member. It felt heavenly and she knew how to build it up slowly bringing me to a mind blowing climax.

****

The table where I was sitting at was completely surrounded with all the Garntuoas and I still had to get used to the fact that they were naked. I looked at them one by one and I could hardly make out who was older. They all looked very beautiful with their perfectly shaped black lips and beautiful eyes. I was eating a delicious meal and I was communicating with them via my "nerve mate".

They told me that the hover had been completely destroyed and that they had buried two bodies. They were shocked when I told them what had happened on the hover and didn't blame me for the death of the pilot.

I was relieved that I had survived the crash and I actually needed to contact the main city. My nerve mate told me that I needed to talk to the elder and that everything would be handled by her.

I agreed and after I had said good bye to the other Garntuoas my nerve mate left me to fetch the elder.

I was taken aback when the elder walked into the room. It was the first time I had seen her in daylight and she looked exactly like Laura except the colour of her eyes. They were bright blue and as soon as she began speaking I could hear she was related to Laura. She said, "It seems that the Garntuoas really like you."

"Yes it seems so. Are you and Laura sisters?"

She gasped and said, "How dare you to call The Highest by her name!"

I smiled and said with confidence, "Since she asked me to do so."

She huffed, "I can't believe that my sister would do such a thing."

I sighed and I said, "Please, I'm not here to upset you. I just want a ride back so I can proceed with the regeneration ceremony."

The elder laughed softly and said, "This *is* the regeneration. It is the regeneration of the Garntuoa gene chain."

I was dumbstruck.

It was never about my own regeneration! I had the silly notion that they would regenerate my memory.

I felt suddenly scared, and whispered, "How did the other men die?"

She said placidly, "They couldn't deal with the Garntuoa's body fluids. It was too poisonous for them. You survived because you are practically Garntuoa."

Then it dawned on me why Laura had insisted that I remove the ring from my cock: I wouldn't have any healthy sperm. The cryptic speech Laura had given before I went to her made sense as well: you were allowed to stay and become a Yourien citizen after you had delivered your part of the regeneration of the gene.

Now I understood what the healing master had been trying to tell me. He knew the Garntuoa's body fluids would be poisonous for a normal human being but not for me.

I blew out some air.

It all was clear except for one thing and I asked, "How is it possible that Estrella is Laura's daughter? I know that Estrella was carried in the womb of a Garntuoa."

Her face darkened and she said, "It was the biggest offering the Garntuoas made. As The Highest you can't bear a child but for the bloodline it was necessary. One of the Garntuoas offered to carry the fertilised egg knowing she probably wouldn't survive. She died on the very day that we took Estrella out of her womb."

I felt horrible and utterly shocked knowing that they had lost one of their few survivors. My nerve mate sat next to me and when she got the picture her eyes filled with tears.

I hugged her trying to comfort her and the elder said softly, "It was her mother."

My nerve mate crawled into my lap and I rocked her softly feeling awful knowing I had ripped open old wounds.

She showed me a picture of me and Estrella holding a baby boy and I knew that it was of some comfort to her that the end of the long and painful quest of the regeneration was finally in sight.

****

I was sitting together with my nerve mate in the hover traveling back to the city. She had refused to be separated from me and she endured the fact she had to wear a cloak. She snuggled up to me while I held her hand and she was very excited to see the "other world".

I had other expectations and other worries: what was going to happen to me when I returned?

What would the ancient laws describe?

Would I be a Yourien straight away?

How would they react when they saw my nerve mate?

The little hand squeezed mine and she communicated that I was not to worry. That it would all be fine. Her smile was mesmerising when I looked at her pretty face. The hood of her cloak which had a contrasting colour, made her look like a powerful mage and for the first time I could see the real power of a Garntuoa.

The hover descended which meant we were nearly there and she moved her hood over her head. Her black gloves made her a completely mysterious small figure which exuded sophistication.

The hover landed and I hated that the hatch opened so slowly. The sun shone straight in my eyes when I stepped out the hover and I was completely taken aback when I heard the deafening cheer coming from the gathered crowd.

I moved a few steps forward out of the blinding sun and saw everyone standing there. I saw Estrella, Ellonary,

The healing master and Theodor amongst the crowd.

Laura stood on a small platform just a few feet away from me and her smile reached her eyes.

My nerve mate was still behind me but when Laura started to speak she moved next to me, "Xander, welcome back. I have the honour of handing you your official Yourien identity card. Your regeneration ceremony has successfully come to an end."

I saw a twinkle in her eyes when my nerve mate took my hand and she said, "I think you need some time to prepare yourself for the dinner I have organised but I hope I will see you there."

I bowed and I said, "It will be my honour to be there Your Highest."

She smiled and said, "Good. My Fille will escort you to your quarters."

My heart skipped a beat. Laura openly allowed Estrella to escort me. I bet she knew already what had needed to be done to save the Garntuoas from extinction. I bowed deeply and said, "Thank You Your Highest."

Laura stepped down from the platform and handed me a small card which looked like it was made of plastic. As soon as I took it from her it changed from the dull white to a deep red colour and my face appeared including a few numbers at the card. Beneath my picture was my name Xander.

Laura smiled. "Take good care of it."

"I will Your Highest."

All this time my nerve mate was holding my arm and I could see Laura looking at her as if she wanted to know who she was. Laura said softly, "I have spoken with my sister and I have heard you have some revealing news for me. I would like to have a talk with you before dinner."

I replied, "As you wish Your Highest. I assume your Fille can bring me to your quarters?"

Her warm smile made me at ease and she said, "That would be wonderful."

Estrella stood between me and her mother and she said, "Okay, but first let me take you to your new quarters."

Laura chuckled, "Off you go my Fille."

Estrella took my hand and we walked away from the crowd. As soon as we were clear from the crowd she kissed me passionately on my lips and whispered, "By Yourian, I never thought I could suffer so much. Eight cycles! Eight very long and scary cycles!"

I hugged her and I said softly, "I'm sorry you had to suffer that long."

She sighed, "The healing master said you would survive because of your Garntuoa nerves but he had no idea why it took so long."

I suddenly felt stupid because I totally had forgotten that my nerve mate was with me and I quickly looked around to see where she was. To my relief she was standing just a few feet away from me and she had taken down her hood. The twinkle in her eyes told me she wasn't upset. I cleared my throat and I said to Estrella while I was pointing at my nerve mate, "Estrella I want to you meet someone and I think you know her already."

Estrella squeaked with happiness and rushed over to the beaming Garntuoa. She lifted my nerve mate in her arms and chanted, "Oh, Monova. Monova, I have missed you so much."

The two women were crying from joy and I was surprised to hear that my nerve mate had a name: Monova, a strong name which fitted her perfectly.

When Estrella had calmed a bit she asked, "Why is Monova with you?"

"She is my nerve donor and we have a special bond. She is going to stay with me, uh, us."

Monova gestured for me to join the hug and when I did I felt her enormous joy. Estrella said softly, "Let's go to your new home."

CHAPTER FOURTEEN.

When I opened the door of my new quarters a small cheer erupted from the room: Ellonary, Laura and the healing master were there already. I knew now why Estrella had kissed me right in the corridor.

My eyes shot directly to Ellonary. She looked so fantastic, so fresh, and so healthy! She rushed over to me and hugged me firmly. Her eyes were filled with tears when she kissed me lightly on my lips before saying with a quivering voice, "Welcome back Xander. My hero."

I saw joy but also the grief in her eyes. She had clearly been hurt very badly. I felt happy to have her in my arms again and I caressed her back while I whispered in her ear, "Oh Ellonary I have missed you so much. I'm so happy that you are here."

We stood there enjoying the tender hug and while she laid her head on my shoulder she said softly, "Don't dare leave me alone for such long period again! Promise me."

I chuckled while looking at Laura, "I promise, next time I'll take you with me."

Laura knelt down to Monova with tears running down her cheeks and she said hoarsely, "Monova."

Monova took Laura's face gently in her hands and

kissed her on her forehead and had a warm smile. Her hand sought mine as if she wanted me to be her interpreter. I let go of Ellonary to kneel down as well and I took her hand.

I saw a trail of images which I tried to translate as accurately as possible and I had trouble putting them into the right context. I cleared my throat because I was affected by Laura's emotions. I knew she felt guilty for the death of Monova's mother.

I said with a somewhat croaky voice, "Monova has never blamed you for her mother's death. It was her mother's choice and she wants you to know that her mother never had any regrets."

Monova hugged her and Laura whispered, "Thank you Monova, my Monova. But why are you here?"

I said, "Monova is my nerve mate. She is the one who donated the nerve solution to me and we are bonded to each other."

Ellonary and the healing master said in unison, "That is unbelievable."

Monova showed me that it was time to tell Laura what had happened.

I knew it was for Laura and Estrella only and I said, "I have an important message from the elder to Estrella and her mother."

The healing master instantly understood what I wanted and taking Ellonary by the hand, he said "Come Ellonary it is time to get ready. I'll take you to your room so you can prepare for the dinner party."

She chuckled and purred, "I'm going to wear something smoking hot I can't wait to show it to you."

I couldn't let this one go and I said with a funny smile, "I'm looking forward to that Ellonary but the fountain is mine."

Laura and Ellonary burst out laughing and when I saw that Ellonary didn't get my joke I said to her, "This one is for our late night stories."

Ellonary said with a mesmerising smile while walking out of the door with the healing master, "I'll get you for this, some day."

When the door had closed I took a deep breath and said, "Let's sit on the bed so I can tell you what has happened and what needs to happen soon."

****

Estrella and Monova were snuggled up to me. Laura had left after I had told her the entire story because she had to go to prepare herself for the dinner.

Laura and Estrella were flabbergasted and thrilled to hear that the regeneration scheme of the Garntuoas was nearly complete. Estrella couldn't believe that she and I were involved in piecing together the final parts of the genes to finish the long quest.

I knew for sure that Estrella needed some more time to realise what was expected from us but her mother did. She looked at me with a funny smirk knowing that she would be grandma soon. I was very pleased that Laura had taken the news with a sense of pride for Estrella.

Estrella stroked my hair and said, "Do you believe in destiny?"

I chuckled, "You mean that you picked me up from another planet and now we are the key to regenerating the right gene?"

She was silent for a moment and said, "Yes, something like that."

I certainly had second thoughts about those off the wall belief systems but what had happened to me was far-out as well.

I hesitated for a moment and then I conceded, "Considering everything that has happened, yes I'm willing to believe it."

She giggled. "You are so funny."

Monova crawled over me to Estrella and started to

sniff her skin like a dog. She licked the crease of Estrella's arm and brought her nose above Estrella's lips.

Estrella remained rigid the whole time and sighed with relief when Monova giggled.

Monova took my hand and I couldn't believe what she showed me and I whispered, "How is that possible?"

Estrella was getting nervous and asked with a small voice, "Is something wrong?"

Taking my hand Monova insisted that I ask Estrella her question. Happy to oblige I said, "Monova asked if your breasts are sensitive."

Estrella's face turned bright red, automatically moving her hands to her breasts and nodding slowly.

It must have happened on the afternoon that we went to visit Ellonary. She had insisted on having me inside her and even though I had full control over my orgasm, there must have been enough living sperm in my pre cum to have impregnated her. I still had trouble fathoming what had happened but I felt strangely excited. I tried to clear my throat but I still croaked a little when I said, "It seems you're pregnant."

She sat up and whispered, "Oh dear. What am I going to do?"

I hadn't expected her to react like that but Monova and I hugged her gently and I said trying to calm her, "I'm thrilled we are having a child."

Estrella smiled but then her face turned ashen and whispered, "What if it's a girl?"

Monova sent me a picture of my erect cock. I saw the humour of it and I had trouble keeping my voice as normal as possible when I retorted, "Monova says it's a boy." I glared into Monova's eyes and she had trouble not giggling.

Estrella sighed, "What am I going to say to my mom?"

I took her hand, "Nothing yet. It's too early."

She looked down and sighed. "All right."

I asked her, "Estrella, are you really ready to have a

baby?"

She looked up and said, "Only if you going to stay here... with me, so we can raise the child together."

I understood that she wanted my commitment. I still had the freedom to opt to leave the planet but I felt I had no reason to go back. I didn't even know what would happen to me if I did.

Here I had three wonderful women who I deeply cared for and I kissed her softly on her lips. Having a child of my own blood made the decision to stay easier and I murmured jokingly, "The boy needs a real man to survive all those strong women."

She slapped me but playfully purred, "Hmmm, muscle guy. Let's get ready for dinner."

****

We were all dressed and ready for the special dinner. Monova was dressed in a black gown which was beautifully decorated with rows of diamonds and I started to wonder who she really was. I suspected that she held a high status.

I took her hands and I asked, "I have a suspicion that you are somebody special."

She chuckled and showed pictures of a little girl.

"I know you're a beautiful girl. But you're more than just a little girl."

Her face became a little darker, which must have been a blush, when she showed me an image of her mother together with her father sitting on a throne in a huge hall filled with Garntuoas who were bowing to them. She was a member of the royal family and now the Queen of the Garntuoas. I instantly had even more respect for her late mother for choosing to carry Estrella in her womb. Estrella had been surrounded with royal Garntuoa blood and now Monova had shared her nerves with a total stranger. Okay, it seemed that my manipulated DNA together with Estrella's would be the new future for the Garntuoas but she couldn't have known that.

I blew out some air and I said, "Now I understand why the elder made such a fuss."

Monova giggled and showed me that all Garntuoas were supportive of her decision. I knew that she couldn't stay in the city and that she had to go back in the foreseeable future.

Estrella stood watching us with a broad smile and she said, "I wasn't allowed to tell you that she was the Queen of the Garntuoas but I'm impressed at how quickly you found out."

I wanted to retort, but Theodor stood in the opening of the door.

"Laura insisted that I had to escort you to the dinner party."

Estrella harrumphed, "As if the city is full of scum."

Theodor said, "We still don't know who killed BB."

I gasped and I said apologetically, "It was the other introduced who killed BB. He was proud of the fact that he had murdered her because she was too good. I'm so glad he's no threat anymore."

"What happened to him?"

I was surprised that he didn't know what had happened and I said, "We had a fight in the hover and he killed the pilot. The hover started to tilt and I fell out. By grabbing tree tops I got myself down safely. The hover however crashed with a huge explosion and according to the Garntuoas they didn't survive the inferno because they buried two bodies."

"Interesting news. Strange that I should hear that from you."

I didn't know why it hadn't reached him but I was not really fussed about it and I said, "Oh, I'm sure you will get the news sooner or later."

Theodor sighed, "I guess I will but I still don't understand how Max managed to get this man on the planet."

I suddenly remembered that the sponsor had given the midget a knife and I asked Theodor, "What happened to the sponsor?"

There was a short silence and he said calmly, "I killed him."

"Oh?"

"He was angry at me and he drew his knife. He made the mistake of throwing it to me."

I was intrigued and I asked, "What happened?"

He said calmly, "I deflected the knife and unfortunately it ended up right in his heart."

I was actually very pleased and I said dryly, "Gosh, indeed how unfortunate."

I saw Theodore smiling and he said, "After the celebrations we should have a talk Alex."

I knew he wanted me on his team and I felt honoured. I smirked when I said, "Yes, I think we should."

As we entered the hall a voice shouted, "The Queen of the Garntuoas! The Fille of The Highest!"

I sighed. I was walking in between Monova and Estrella and all eyes were on us again. We stopped in front of Laura who looked very relaxed and when we had bowed to her she paid her respect to Monova by bowing deeply towards her.

Laura said with a strong voice which seemed to carry through the whole hall, "Today is a memorable day. We are honoured to receive Queen Monova, ruler of the Garntuoas and the man who successfully returned from the regeneration, Alex."

The audience applauded loudly while a few men shouted "Youria!". When the noise died down Laura continued, "We will celebrate as we enter a new era in our history of this planet: The chapter of the rebirth of the Garntuoas. After countless periods we, together with the Garntuoas, have finally built the right gene sequence to let the population of the Garntuoas grow."

There were loud cheers which died down quickly when Laura held up her arm. She looked around when she spoke again, "Many know the dreadful history and the pledge we took to keep on working to save the Garntuoas and now we can celebrate the success. I invite you all to join me at the grand dinner festival. May it all become to you well."

The Highest walked down her raised platform and strode to the adjacent hall.

CHAPTER FIFTEEN.

I felt a hand take my hand and as I turned I saw Ellonary standing next to me beaming like a little school girl. It was a funny view seeing her looking so excited while she was dressed in a smoking hot gown. It showed all her beautiful feminine curves and I was sure she was naked under her dress because I couldn't see any bits of fabric which looked like underwear. I was pleased that it wasn't see-through but it still made me look twice.

I whispered in her ear, "By Yourian, you look amazingly hot!"

She purred, "Thanks! Using our planet's name already?"

She was right: I wasn't really aware of it when I said it but somehow it felt right. I conceded, "I picked it from Estrella and I thought it sounded interesting."

She chuckled while she squeezed my hand and said, "I swapped places so I can sit next to you. Monova is opposite you and Estrella is seated on the other side of you."

I smiled realising I was going to have a triangle of the women I liked and I said, "Who was sitting next to me before you did your little swap?"

"The elder. The sister of The Highest."

Relieved I squeezed her hand to thank her and I whispered in her ear, "Perfect! Thanks!"

****

Ellonary and I were strolling in the gardens of the city. Estrella had more or less commanded me to spend the night with Ellonary. She used the excuse that she needed some time together with Monova to discuss her current state. It then dawned on me that she could communicate the same way with Monova as me. The only thing I didn't understand is why Monova didn't tell Estrella directly that she was pregnant.

Ellonary's sigh brought me out of my thoughts and I squeezed her hand.

She hugged me and said, "When I came to I was so scared that you had gone to the regeneration ceremony without saying goodbye."

I caressed her back and I kissed her neck gently. I shivered, "When I saw you laying on the bed completely covered in blood I felt so useless. We had to wait for the protective sheet before we could go in. I was so pleased when I heard you were still alive."

She moved away from me so that she could look into my eyes and quivered, "All I remember is Max trying to rip my clothes off, and that I managed to kick him in his groin. After that I felt a blow against my temple which knocked me out completely."

I unintentionally squeezed my legs together when I recalled how painful a powerful kick in your balls can be. She blew out some air and said with a tremble in her voice, "I never thought that Max would do something like that."

I stroked her cheek as I said, "It seems that he had never dealt with the loss of his job. It backfired on him very badly."

Her eyes looked very sad and she asked, "Will you stay

the night with me?"

I felt the urge to comfort her and I hugged her softly when I said, "Yes, I'd love to Ellonary."

We walked slowly back to her room and when she closed the door she said, "You know, I feel safe with you and I can let it be. Being the hot naughty nurse isn't always that much fun."

I realised that it was her way of dealing with what had happened to her and I said reassuringly, "Ellonary please be yourself and tell me what you want."

Her lips trembled a bit and she asked softly, "Do you think you can make love to me?"

I looked at her and I saw a woman who needed to be cherished, to be nurtured, to be pampered and a whole host of other things to make her feel wonderful.

I took her face between my hands and I kissed her full lips as tenderly as I could. A tear ran down her cheek and as I kissed the tear away I pulled her in my arms.

I whispered in her ear, "Oh Ellonary, my lovely Ellonary."

****

I spent more than an hour admiring her body by kissing and stroking it softly. She had been close to an orgasm several times but I had prevented it from happening. Her whole body was practically trembling with anticipation when I finally entered her. I stayed inside her because she wanted to be as close as possible to me. After many tender kisses we started to move slowly and Ellonary reached a very gently but emotional climax which lasted for minutes. Eventually she dragged me into her everlasting emotional bliss and I never had such a powerful yet physically gentle orgasm.

It had drained us completely and we both fell into a satisfied sleep.

I woke up because someone was tracing a finger over my chest. I felt a leg sliding over my legs and I heard a sigh of contentment. Two lips were pressed on my arm and a luscious soft body pressed against my side.

I moaned softly when a hand caressed my hardening member. I opened my eyes and I saw Ellonary's beautiful eyes looking lustfully at me.

She whispered, "I always wanted to do this."

I smiled and I sighed. "This is a very nice way to wake up."

I heard the ring beep twice and I smiled when I remembered yesterday evening. I had nearly forgotten I didn't have a ring and we were lucky that Ellonary had a spare in one of her drawers.

I looked at her with a questioning look. She kissed me long but very gentle. She nipped at my nose and said, "I'm not really in the mood for a fast one."

I was not really surprised and I asked jokingly, "No quickie then?"

She laughed and sat up when she said, "No, no quickie today because we need to be at Estrella's for breakfast. Come I'll wash your back in the shower."

I sighed with bliss because I knew now that I was going to be pampered by three women who all wanted to spend time with me.

I started to wonder if I would ever enjoy them all at the same time. All I knew for now was that a lot would change rapidly:

Estrella being pregnant, Monova couldn't stay in the city forever and Ellonary who needed to recover from her traumatic experience.

I came suddenly to a solution which might appeal to all parties: Build a house close to the Garntuoa enclave which was big enough for the four of us including future children as well as being able to host Laura and her team.

EPILOGUE.

I was sitting on the rocking chair at the veranda of my house trying to get my grandson to sleep. He was one of the first real Garntuoa males ever born after the chemical war. He was as red as Monova and his body was the right proportion for the Garntuoas.

I was very pleased that the gene combinations of Estrella and me had created the semi-Garntuoa children whereby the males were able to conceive hundred percent Garntuoa offspring.

Just before the chemical cloud hit the main Garntuoa enclave they managed to save an enormous amount of Garntuoa egg cells. Together with our sons and grandsons we would form the roots of the new race of Garntuoas.

****

I was a sole survivor of the regeneration ceremony which had a twist that I heard just a few years, periods, ago.

Estrella wanted to study other planets where human-like species were living and she had chosen to visit my planet.

She had an accident when trying to travel back to her own planet. She lost her vessel which I apparently had found and I had managed to get one of her devices to work.

The combination of me using the device and her new travel device triggered the lightning which struck me in my chest.

Was it destiny? Who knows? All I knew was that it had brought me here to this planet where I was living with Estrella, Ellonary and my Garntuoa nerve mate Monova in a house close to the Garntuoa tribe.

I was happy living with them. It was only made possible after saving the main city of Youria. We'd paid a high price but it had been worth it.

****

Ellonary walked up to me and said softly, "If the little one is asleep you have to come to your room."

I looked at her smile and then she whispered in my ear, "It's your regeneration day."

That brought a huge smile on my face as I knew I was going to enjoy the afternoon with three women in my bed.

ABOUT THE AUTHOR

Kin Asdi (aka Victor Vergeer), was born in 1964 and raised in the Netherlands. He is happily married and lives with his wife and teenage daughter in a village on the outskirts of The Hague, the Netherlands. He studied Sonology (the science of sound) at the Royal Conservatoire in The Hague where he learned to appreciate a wide range of music and other creative arts that involved the use of sound. His particular talent was for human interfaces, something he specializes in even today; interfaces being the creative link between man and technology. His passion for computers and programming began as a boy when his father introduced him to the world of bits and bytes. Today he earns his living as an HR programmer working with interfaces and getting the technology to meet the needs of the customer!

In his free time he has always been involved with creative activities varying from building speakers and furniture, to creating coloured light objects using LEDs and electronics. He likes to create unique objects, and constantly seeks new challenges to push back the boundaries of his own knowledge and satisfy his curiosity about the world.

Reading a lot of indie-published books made him aware of the 'new' way of writing and publishing.

It was then that he discovered how much he enjoys writing stories: something which provides another outlet for a creative mind. He was surprised to discover that, for him, writing is both demanding and relaxing. The differences between programming and creative writing are actually surprisingly small. Whether you are writing a program or a story, you need a structured framework; a beginning, a middle and an end, all of which has to flow and make sense in order for it to work.

Being able to put his imagination to work and express his ideas in words has opened a new chapter in his life. He published his first young adult sci-fi adventure novel last year and the second is currently in preparation. He finds it very rewarding that others like to read what he has written, which gives him the encouragement to continue to explore the world of creative writing.